artforms. A beautiful collection of strange and unsettling stories from Scotland's past, present and possible futures."
Katy Lennon, *Blood Bath Literary Zine*

"*Haunted Voices* occupies an important Gothic corner in the Scottish storytelling tradition, drawing on Scotland's rich oral history while being at the forefront of something new. *Haunted Voices* spans Scotland's urban and remote landscapes to put its finger firmly on the pulse of a well established (and continuing) oral storytelling culture. The supernatural themes send shivers down the spine and showcase the vitality of the Scottish storytelling tradition. Spellbinding."
thatbloodywomanreads

An Anthology of
Gothic Storytelling from Scotland

PUBLISHING

Published by Haunt Publishing
www.hauntpublishing.com
@HauntPublishing

'The Keep' by Kirsty Logan was first published in *A Portable Shelter*, published by the Association for Scottish Literary Studies in 2015.

'the possession' by Sean Wai Keung uses material from the Wikipedia articles https://en.wikipedia.org/wiki/Hungry_ghost and https://en.wikipedia.org/wiki/Greenbank_Garden which are released under Creative Commons Attribution-Share-Alike License 3.0.

ISBN: 978-1-9162347-0-3
ebook: 978-1-9162347-1-0
Audiobook: 978-1-9162347-2-7

Cover design and illustrations: Zuzanna Kwiecien
Typesetter: Laura Jones
Editor: Rebecca Wojturska

Printed and bound in Great Britain by Clays Ltd, Elcograf S.p.A.

CONTENTS

INTRODUCTION

Boo! Welcome to *Haunted Voices*.

I'd love to pretend that the idea for an anthology that celebrates Gothic oral storytelling came to me in a monstrous, Mary Shelley-esque dream, but sadly it did not. It came from trips as a bairn into the fringes of the misty Highlands and spooky experiences of watching local storytellers recite chilling local legends.

It was the combination of these experiences and my first trip to Edinburgh – I passed a building called the Scottish Storytelling Centre and noticed spooky tour guides coming in and out of the shadowy closes – that confirmed for me that Scotland's oral storytelling culture is very much alive and present, if only you know where to look, or where to listen.

Research revealed the richness, breadth and distinctiveness of Scotland's oral tradition and eventually led me to the University of Edinburgh's School of Scottish Studies Archives, a hidden gem of huge cultural importance that includes, among a wealth of material recording and preserving Scottish folklore and traditional arts, audio-recordings of past storytelling masters. Headphones on and wonderstruck, it was a privilege to hear members of now legendary Traveller and storytelling families sharing their tales. (It has been an even greater privilege that members of this community, and the archive itself, have granted me permission to reproduce these stories and let me share them yet further.)

It was apparent, however, that the oral tradition wasn't only the stuff of archives: it is alive and thriving in the present, with magnificent storytellers performing across the country in the very same mode, continuing the tradition.

And its legacy doesn't stop there. Like so many art forms, oral storytelling is shapeshifting in the modern world, drifting ghostlike into unexpected places, as technologies and changing cultural practices open new oral spaces. Just click on a podcast app, or drop by a spoken word night, or walk into a tent at a music festival... Scotland is buzzing with oral storytelling.

Haunted Voices sets out to do several things:

- To celebrate Scotland's oral storytelling culture. To shine a light on its rich history, contemporary storytellers continuing in the traditional mode and the tradition's influence on those working in emerging oral spaces.

- To do so in both text and audio, making the collected tales as accessible as possible, and to maximise their reach. Some people are unable to attend live storytelling events (for whatever reason) and this should not leave oral culture inaccessible. *Haunted Voices* brings oral storytelling into the home of anyone who welcomes it in, urging it vampire-like over their threshold. Or into the cabin in the woods they've rented with friends looking for a scare. Or across the sea and into the homes of international readers and listeners who shouldn't need to purchase a flight to Scotland to discover what its oral storytelling culture has to offer.

- To reflect the diversity of voices in Scotland. *Haunted Voices* celebrates regional diversity (voices from Aberdeen, the Borders, Dundee, Edinburgh, Fife, Glasgow, the Highlands, Orkney, Skye and elsewhere), LGBTQI+ voices, voices of people of colour and voices from those rich points of intersection where Scotland's traditional arts meet those of other cultures.

- To create more storytelling opportunities in Scotland for both performers and audiences. *Haunted Voices* launched with a programme of inexpensive or free live events, with an eye on organising further events in future.

- To celebrate the Gothic.

Why the Gothic? First, the Gothic is my true literary love. And second, Scotland is renowned for its deep and longstanding affinity with that most unsettling of genres. So much so, in fact, that around the globe people debate the existence of a form of the Gothic unique to Scotland (known as – wait for it – Scottish Gothic). So, it was no hard task to find archived tales dealing with themes familiar to the Gothic: death and decay;

doublings and doppelgängers; the uncanny; abuses of inherited power, especially religious or patriarchal; and, of course, hauntings, be they supernatural or psychological. Nor was it a challenge to find contemporary storytellers crafting wonderfully disturbing Gothic tales.

But the purpose of *Haunted Voices* – and, in fact, the founding purpose of Haunt Publishing – is not to gatekeep the Gothic; it is not to define and limit what the Gothic is, what the Gothic does, what the Gothic can do. In fact, it is the very opposite: it is to leave the graveyard gates wide open and watch old forms crawl into the present. To let the Gothic roam where it will, twisting itself into shapes horrible and unseen. To wait for it to open its ancient mouth and to listen – to listen to what this age-old thing has to tell us about the terrors and wonders of our world.

So, gather round the hearth, or light a candle, and enjoy these tales of terror from some of the most talented oral storytellers in Scotland.

Rebecca Wojturska, Editor

A NOTE ON ARCHIVE MATERIAL

Several of the stories in this anthology are reproduced from the University of Edinburgh's School of Scottish Studies Archives. The School of Scottish Studies Archives preserves material related to Scottish folklore, cultural traditions and traditional arts.

The audio recordings of the following stories have been reproduced with permission from the University of Edinburgh's School of Scottish Studies Archives, the storytellers' families and the fieldworkers or fieldworkers' families. Titles have been added for the purposes of this anthology.

A Graveyard Wager
Duncan Williamson recorded by Dr Linda Williamson in 1976 (tape ID: SA1976.209).

The Fire and the Factor
Jeannie Robertson recorded by Hamish Henderson in 1954 (tape ID: SA1954.090).

The Man with Two Shadows

Stanley Robertson recorded by Barbara McDermitt in 1982 (tape ID: SA1982.082).

The Skeleton and the Gravestone

Jean Rodger recorded by Dr Emily Lyle in 1976 (tape ID: SA1976.077).

The Warlock and Robbie Ha

Stanley Robertson recorded by Alan J. Bruford in 1978 (tape ID: SA1978.013).

The Wee Singing Bird

Betsy Whyte recorded by Alan J. Bruford in 1981 (tape ID: SA1981.063).

The transcriptions in this anthology of these stories are original, i.e. are not reproduced from the University of Edinburgh's School of Scottish Studies Archives. The transcribing process is not an exact science and the transcriptions therefore represent one interpretation of the audio material and do not necessarily reproduce the material with complete accuracy.

To listen to more archived recordings from the School of Scottish Studies, visit: www.tobarandualchais.co.uk.

THE WARLOCK AND ROBBIE HA

Stanley Robertson

This is a story my granda telt us when I was a bairn. And for years and years it used to terrify me. And I think that's responsible for me getting these funny sensations now! There's nothing like the power of imagination. You couldna sleep! You started to fall asleep – what? Help!

There's an old legend in Scotland – it's common among the Robertsons and common among the MacDonalds; it's common throughout all of Scotland in fact – that when a person dies they become the keeper of the grave. It's also common to believe, in Scotland, that if you are the last of your generation you become a crying banshee. It's believed amongst the travelling people. This is one of the beliefs that all the travelling people had; a very common belief.

This story is about a man cried Robbie Ha. My granda used to tell us this story, and Robbie Ha got this name because he grew a big, fat, sticking-out belly. Usually the word ha, when you used the word ha, it meant a big hunger – you were a body who ate a lot – but this man got this name simply because he had this big protruding belly. Now, he lived up in Inverness-shire way, about a hundred years ago, and he used to be a tinsmith. He lived nearly all summer by sharpening shears and mending pots and pans. And he was good, he said: he could do odd jobs here, there and everywhere. In the wintertime he would usually seek lodgings inside, and he used to keep the money he made in the summer to last him through the winter, and he would do odd jobs for folk as well, in the towns, but it was mostly up north. He liked being out in the camp and going round the wee towns and villages.

This time, somewhere about Inverness-shire way – I think it was right near the west of Inverness-shire – when he was up there this time, he comes to a wee townie, and it was summertime. And in this wee townie – it was a fairly thriving wee community townie – he says, "Ach, I'll do some business here, I'll probably get a few jobs to do." He noticed a big house awa in the distance, and he says, "Och," he says, "I'll try this house," he says, "that looks like a fine big house. Houses that big usually give you something; if you get a job to do from them you get a *good* job. And they're maybe like to give you a job sorting silver or something, things they couldna actually get done unless they brought it to places like Glasgow or Inverness or that." So, he says, "I'll have a go here." He knocks at the door, and a servant answers it, this servant lassie. He says, "Is there any work here?" He tells her what he does.

"Look," she says, "you maybe could assist," she says. "It just so happens that there's a death in this house just now. You could assist the undertaker, because for some reason his assistants are off." And Robbie says, "Is there nobody to help him?" She says, "I dinna want to help him because I dinna really work here, I'm only here for the day. But you can come in and help him." So, the undertaker comes to the door. He wasna dressed like undertakers nowadays; the man was just dressed in ordinary clothes. And the undertaker kent this man and he says, "Oh, aye, aye. Robbie. I'm glad to see you. If you come in and help me to do this job, I'll give you thirty shillings." And that was a good skelp of money to do a job. And Robbie says, "Oh, for thirty shillings I'll do anything." So, he comes in. He looks round this house and it was the strangest-looking house he ever did see. The walls all didna seem right – everything seemed to be off balance – and there were strange-looking mirrors and strange designs. He says, "What a weird-looking house this is."

He comes to a room, and here lying in the bed was the most horrific corpse he had ever seen. It was half sitting up and it was all twisted and convulsed, and the hands were all knotted and twisted, and it had this horrible expression – hideous – as though someone had really died in hideous agony. And Robbie says, "Oh, my, that poor man looks dreadful." And the under-taker says, "Aye, he's no enough a bonnie sight. Rigor mortis has set in. I've got his coffin up and that, but we'll need to, ken, break his bones and that to get him in. He winna lie like this." Because he was all twisted.

So, they did what they did to get him in the box.

When they got him in the box the undertaker says, "Accordingly, he's going to get a funeral tomorrow. There'll be no long wait or anything. He has very few friends. And this old man never was fond of me." And Robbie says, "Well, I never kent that old man."

When he came out from the work he says, "That was a hideous job to do." The undertaker says to him, "Come down to the shop and I'll give you the money." He didna have the money on him. So, Robbie goes out and does one or two wee jobs and, later on, he comes down by the undertaker's shop. It was a small business, but that had been the biggest townie of the area, and probably did for all the community. And as he comes to this undertaker's shop he notices two laddies there. Robbie says to them, "Are you no the undertaker's assistants?" And one says, "No." He says, "You're awfa like them. I'm sure I've seen yous working." And they says, "Oh, we really are, but we wouldna work up there in that house. That old man was a warlock. And we werena having no dealings with an old warlock. No, no." And they says, "When he died, he died screaming that loud that his screams could be heard in the village." You see, the house was just outside the village. And they says, "The screams of this man could be heard. It was really eerie."

The undertaker's name was Mr James. And this Mr James, there had been bad blood between him and the old warlock. And Robbie says, "Well, what was the bad blood between them?" One boy says, "Well, there was a young skiffy lassie came to work in the warlock's house. And the warlock was corrupting her. The warlock liked this lassie, but he was going to use her for all kind of practices and get her involved in things she shouldna have been in with." They were awfully religious kind of folk up there. And he says, "Mr James put her right, gave her some money, and got her awa back to Glasgow. So, she was took awa. And the warlock never forgave him for this. And when the warlock died, he died cursing the undertaker. And his last words were that if he could get Mr James, he would come back from the grave and get him.

Robbie says, "That's a horrible thing to say; a horrible story."

Robbie comes down to the shop and the undertaker says, "Here's your money," and gives him the thirty shillings. So, Robbie goes awa and he buys himself a couple of bottles of whisky. "I've had enough," he says, and he goes awa back. And as he went out the back of the townie there was a wee graveyard, just out at the side of the road. And up a bittie from the grave-yard there was a burn and a wood, and that's where Robbie had his camp. So, he went in there, and he has a dram, and he's no really thinking of it, so he has a good drink and he falls asleep all night, and that was okay. He wakens up the next morning, goes into the townie, and he notices the funeral's taking place. There's only about two folk at it. And there wasna a minister at the funeral – this had been the warlock's wish. So, the undertaker couldna get nobody to lower the coffin. The very gravediggers wouldna hardly take part in it. So, he asks Robbie again, and Robbie comes in and helps lower it down into the grave and all that.

When Robbie comes out the graveyard, he feels a dirty cold shiver going up his spine.

That night, when he comes out the pub and goes back to his camp, he has to pass by the graveyard, and he thinks of death and he thinks, "To think that old warlock is buried in there." And he minds the words now that the laddies had telt him, of the story. He comes back to the camp and he's lying in his bed. Ah, but he canna sleep this night, because he's thinking of this horrible old man, and the things that've been said, and he's now tossing and turning. Even the whisky canna put him out now.

He hears, through the night, a voice going:

Ro-bbie…

Ro-bbie…

He says, "There's somebody crying out my name!"

He comes out and he looks down the road. There was a mist – just a rolling mist in the road – and he says, "I canna see nobody on this road."

Ro-bbie…

Ro-bbie…

As he walks nearer, he feels it – it's drawing him nearer to the graveyard. And he hears this voice saying:

Help me, Robbie. Help me.

And he says, "Some poor body's been hurt. They've maybe, ken, fell awa at the side of the graveyard!"

See, you're all right in the graveyard when the keeper's there. But you darena go into the portals of the graves.

When Robbie comes to the graveyard, a thing like a thunderbolt hits him. And he falls down.

He rises up again. But, this time, as this evil old man – the evil spirit has possessed Robbie's body. Robbie's spirit is put unconscious while this evil warlock's spirit comes out and takes over possession of the body now.

It walks back now into the village, right to the wee townie, and in to where the undertaker's shop was. And, of course, undertakers didna lock their doors or that at night because, you ken, folk kent it was all right. So, it opens the first door, gangs up the stairs. The man, the undertaker, had his private door locked and he was in his bed. He wasna married. And this knock comes at the man's door.

Knock.

Knock.

Knock.

The man gets up. He says, "Wha's that?"

He hears, "It's *me.*"

And, of course, he kens Robbie's voice – it was still the same voice, to a point.

He says, "What you needing at this time, Robbie?"

He says, "Let me in."

He opens the door and lets him in. But he notices that his eyes are awfa glazed and *staring* now. And he says to hisself, "Robbie's awfa wild and vicious-looking the night. He's surely had too much to drink and there's something bothering him."

He comes in.

The undertaker sits back in his bed and he says, "Well, what do you want?"

And he just went, *heh, heh, heh* – a horrible, sneering, evil laugh.

Of course, Mr James recognises now the laugh is definitely no the laugh of Robbie. He hears the laugh of the horrible warlock.

There was a box of tools lying just at the side of the table, and this thing puts its hand in and it picks out an awl – a big long awl the undertaker had used for his boxes. And he goes to the undertaker with it.

Now, the undertaker wasna going to let somebody just kill him. So, he gets up to defend hisself. But this evil warlock was in a big, powerful body; the warlock hadna had the build that Robbie Ha had. When the warlock comes to take a hold of him, just at the point when he finally gets the undertaker – he takes this big awl up to stab him – he suddenly hears a scream like a banshee coming in. And the voice roars:

I'VE BEEN CHEATED! I'VE BEEN CHEATED! NO!

Screaming blue murder.

And suddenly, the awl falls out his hand, and Robbie falls to the floor.

Of course, Robbie gives hisself a shock, and he wonders, what on earth is he doing in this man's house? He can obviously see that this man is upset, that he's been attacked or something. He says to him, "Look," he says, "I'm awfa – I dinna ken, I must have been awfa awfa drunk. The last thing I remember was going to help somebody at the graveyard."

The undertaker opens a bottle of brandy and gives hisself some brandy and gives Robbie some brandy. They start to speak about the old legend in Scotland. He says, "Well, that old warlock said he would come back, but something must have prevented him at the last minute. He had the power," he says; "he used you, you were the sort of medium by which he came through, but he didna have the power to finish off the deed." And they were speaking for maybe about an hour; an hour passed by. And then a laddie came in the shop. He says, "Mr James," he says, "that's old Morag in the glen just passed awa."

Old Morag took a place as the keeper of the grave, and she cancelled the other one out.

And that's the story of Robbie Ha.

Have you heard that before? It's weird. You'll have to look up your archives and see if you hear any more stories about it!

THE HOUSE

Seoras Macpherson

Everyone in the glen knew The House. It was never named or identified by its croft number, as others were. It was a nice-looking house, with big bay windows to its ground floor rooms and a beautiful view down the glen to the sea. A house that caught and smiled with the sun. Yet when you passed it, even on a bright warm day, you could feel cold fingers touch the back of your neck, and your hair moved. If you were taking a horse past The House, it would shy away from it, and try to go to the side of the road farthest from The House.

A young man and his wife had come to the glen and fallen in love with the beautiful landscape. They decided it was the place they wanted to live and bought a croft on which they built The House. They appeared to be a happy couple. The man was thought to be from a Scandinavian country and was referred to as 'the Viking' by some in the glen. His wife was Scottish and had relations not far from the glen.

Not long after they moved into their new house, the wife

disappeared. When people asked where she was, her husband said she had left early in the morning to walk across the hill to visit a relation, which was quite a usual thing in those days. However, when the time turned from days to weeks, more questions were asked, including by the husband, and search parties scoured the hill and the route she might have taken, but no sign was found. Suspicion now fell on the husband, and an investigation was held, but no proof could be found of any crime, and there was no body, so the husband was cleared.

He lived alone in The House for a few months but then left the glen and put The House up for sale. It sold very quickly to a family from near Glasgow, and in due course they moved in to settle in the glen.

It was a surprise to everyone when, after a short time in The House, they suddenly returned to Glasgow, claiming that country life didn't suit them. Once again, The House was on the market and sold very quickly, and the new owners moved in. They stayed in The House an even shorter time than the previous owners, and told some of the people in the glen that they were leaving because The House was always cold and unwelcoming. After this The House was sold again several times, but no one stayed in it for more than two weeks. Some only stayed one night.

Now, the ones who had left The House were speaking of weird things that happened in The House. How furniture would move about and crockery would fly off the shelves and shatter on the floor. As its reputation spread it became much harder to sell, and it was tried as a self-catering unit, but this was totally unsuccessful as the people booked into it left after only one or two days, giving various reasons, but mainly telling of the bad feeling, and noises as furniture moved by itself, including one couple who swore that a very heavy chest of drawers full of clothes had moved across the main bedroom by itself, and then the drawers had opened and the contents spilled out. After the failure of this scheme it was sold to a local family at a very low price, and they tried to stay in it because their old house was overcrowded. They spent one night in The House and after that none of them would stay in it nor go into it after dark, and it was used as a store.

An old lady known for her prophecies and her knowledge of supernatural things was taken to The House. She said The House was haunted by a restless spirit who would leave The House when the right people came to it. When they left, she would go with them.

Years went past and no one lived in The House, though some tried, and even leasing it for self-catering was tried again, but The House reacted to this more violently than before. In fact, a family booked it and were shocked by the feeling of evil in The House and by the noises and movement. They decided to leave in the morning, but as they left and their daughter went to push the door shut, the door moved so that their daughter's hand, instead of pushing on the wooden door, pushed on one of the panes of glass in the door, which shattered, cutting her wrist badly.

This was the last time The House was let, and once again it lay empty. After some time, a man and woman came to the glen. They said they were involved in the Black Arts and were looking for a house to buy at a reasonable price. The House was mentioned to them and they liked it and bought it. They lived in it for a year or two and always said what a nice house it was. When they sold it and moved to another house, the people who bought The House were very pleased with The House, and it is now a peaceful, comfortable home.

The old lady said, "I told you when the right people came the restless spirit would leave with them. And it did."

THE RESEARCHER

Fiona Barnett

It is statistically true that when you're the passenger in a car, driving at night along a road outside a city or built-up area, one in four people you see by the side of the road isn't even alive. They've done studies on this sort of thing, you know – if you're ever a passenger on an out-of-the-way road at night, and you see a car coming in the other direction, take a look on the front seat and see if anyone is holding a clipboard. There's a lot of cutting-edge research in this area at the moment, and a lot of it's happening in Scotland, which is pretty exciting. We're at the forefront of something new.

If you do see someone on the side of the road, try not to look them in the eye unless they look at you first. You're probably fine, but it's always good to be a bit cautious. Three times out of four, it won't make any difference at all.

I'm not saying that one in four people by the side of a dark road is a ghost. A ghost is someone who's died, the imprint they leave on the world after they've gone. What you're seeing, more often than not, is someone who never lived in the first place.

They were never a human being – or, rather, they never had a heartbeat and DNA and hair and fingernails that grew. They've always been something else, this other thing.

At the university, just down the road actually, they have a whole research group for studying those beings when they find them. You can't really call them people. They call them wraiths. A lot of the time they just want to find one and photograph it, see which ones come up again and again, check their wellbeing – you know how they put rings around the legs of birds? You can't really do that to a wraith; you can't get that close to them. But if you're really, really lucky, and you manage to stop your car and get out before they disappear, then you might get to talk to one of them.

Now, I used to be a researcher – not in the Wraith Research Group, that's in Psychology; I was round the corner in Linguistics – but I happened to be driving back from Aberdeen with a friend who studies them, about two, two and a half years ago. And we were in the middle of nowhere, and it was about a quarter to one in the morning – that's a thing you get, if you're friends with academics. Never go for dinner with a gastroenterologist – they'll put you right off your food – and never agree to go on a long drive with a wraith psychologist or they'll make you do it at all hours of the night and they'll never take a turn driving.

So, my friend – her name was Rachel – and I were there on the road back from Aberdeen, coming up to one o'clock in the morning, radio off because I was driving and I wanted to concentrate on the road, and suddenly Rachel sits up very straight and says, "Stop the car."

You know I said the proportion is one in four, if you're a passenger? If you're driving the car, you can't see them at all. That's how you know it's a wraith. I didn't really want to stop, I just wanted to get home, but I slammed the brakes on in the middle of the road, and we stopped the car, and Rachel said, "Can you see it?"

And of course I couldn't. If I could, it wouldn't have been an it, it would have been a them – a real person. So, I said, "No. Are you going to get out and do this quickly? Because I want to be in my bed right now."

And Rachel goes, "I'll just be a minute." And she pulled a notebook and pen out of her handbag and got out the car. This was probably February or March, so it was very dark, and pretty cold, and the wind was bitter. She had her coat on, and as she walked out in front of the car, she buttoned it up, and did the hood up. She must have walked maybe ten or twelve yards ahead of the car – and then she stopped, and put her hands up and out, her notebook in one hand. I could hear her say something, but it was over the wind, so I don't know what it was. And then she took a few more steps away, and then a few more, and then a few more, and by this time she was right at the end of what I could see in my headlamps, and she was wearing a dark coat, and I couldn't see her any more.

I sat there watching for a good few minutes, waiting for her to come back. And then the boot of my car opened. I jumped about a foot in the air. But it was Rachel, and her hood was down, and her coat was undone at the front, and she chucked the notebook into the boot of the car, and said, "Only me!", really cheery, like it was the middle of the afternoon and we were waiting in a car park or something, and then she came round to the front seat again and got back in.

So, of course, I said, "Did you find anything?"

And she said, "She's gone, I'm afraid."

And I said, "What was she like?"

And she sort of shrugged, and said, "I'll look at my notes in the morning," and turned the radio on.

And we didn't really speak, all the way back to Edinburgh.

I don't... really... Rachel and I don't really keep in touch these days. She went off to Highlands and Islands a few months later – she got an assistant lecturing job. We were all really proud of her, of course, but even before that she'd thrown herself into her work and we hadn't really spoken in a while. Come to think of it, she didn't speak to the rest of our friends much in those last few months, either. She kept to herself a lot more than she used to. Spent very long hours at the office. I can't really blame her, she did very well – wraith research is quite a niche field and she's one of the leading lights in it. Honestly, she probably knows more about them than almost anyone alive. When you have a calling like that, it's natural that you have to give up a lot of the rest of your life to pursue it. That's just how it works.

But the point is, you just keep an eye out, if you're sat in the passenger seat of a car, driving through the mountains at night. Three times out of four, you're absolutely fine, statistically speaking.

THE LEERIE

Paul Bristow

I don't sleep well, that's the truth of it. I never have.

I don't like the dark. I was ten years old when I finally came to understand why. And nothing has changed my mind since.

I turned ten in 1950, and at this point my exasperated mother decided she could take no more. "A big boy of ten needs to stop worrying about the dark," she kept saying, as if simply saying it would make it so, as if the words would shine bright enough to keep my troubles away.

We were walking home from school, having another of these discussions, when my mother saw a new way to try and convince me I was being silly.

"Look, here's Mr Munro. He knows all about the dark."

Mr Munro was a leerie, one of the few lamplighters left in the town. He was an older man, tall and thin like a gas lamppost himself, with a neat grey beard that did not hide his smile. My mother knew I liked Mr Munro; he always waved when he lit the lamp right outside my bedroom window. She invited him to talk some sense into me.

"Mr Munro? Is there any reason you know of to be afraid of the dark?"

Mr Munro frowned at me, clearly understanding his role in this conversation.

"Not at all. If it wasn't for the dark, I'd not have a job. I make sure there's plenty of light to be had all over the town. And with all these new lamps coming in soon, there won't be a spot of darkness left."

Mr Munro patted me on the head and he and my mother exchanged some gossip about the milkman – a gentleman Mr Munro was not especially fond of.

I stared at his ladder and the pole he used to light the lamps.

If there was no reason to be afraid of the dark, why did we need lamplighters?

That same night, I woke abruptly, into darkness. The lamp outside my window had gone out and the dark had woken me. I scrambled to the window, hoping I would find light elsewhere on the street. All of the lamps were out.

I stared over to the narrow close between the two opposite tenements; there was another gas lamp, which stood right there. Beneath the lamp, standing still, was Mr Munro. He was making no effort to light that lamp, or any of the others; instead, he was staring off down the street towards town.

At first, I supposed that Mr Munro must be performing some maintenance of the lamps, but then I realised that he would surely have done that during the day. I waved to try and get his attention, thinking that I would ask him to light my lamp. If he saw me, he gave no sign, and instead kept watching down the street. I now guessed he must be waiting for a friend or fellow lamplighter. I was mistaken.

Mr Munro seemed to stiffen slightly, pushing himself against the tenement wall. He then bowed his head, as if he were at church. As he did, a shadow passed across the road. I could not make it out properly as the light was so low, but gradually I could see that it was a man, limping slowly across the cobbles, balancing himself on his cane. If Mr Munro knew him, he gave no sign, keeping his head bowed the whole time. The man continued slowly past the lamplighter, into the darkness of the gap between the two buildings. As soon as he had passed, Mr Munro turned his collar up against the cold, gathered the tools of his trade and walked swiftly off down the street. It was over an hour before the streetlamp outside my room was lit again, and all that time I lay thinking about the limping man, and how his cane had made no noise upon the cobbles as he walked.

The next morning, I resolved to investigate the close across the street. I had run in and out of all the tenements and closes in our street, but when I tried to remember this one, I could not. Some closes backed onto others, providing shortcuts through the backstreets; others opened out into courtyards and drying greens. I was surprised and disappointed to find that this one was a dead end, really nothing more than a gap between the buildings. I was not the only person in the close though; Mr Munro was there too, brushing the cobbles.

"Are you looking for your friend?" I asked.

Mr Munro turned with a start, then smiled when he saw it was me.

"It won't do to stay down here too long – not much light, so it gets cold quickly in the winter. You'll catch a chill."

He put his arm on my shoulder and led me back out onto the street.

"How are you getting along at night-time?" he asked.

"Not very well," I said, slightly embarrassed.

"Hmmm. Would you like to know how I came to be a leerie?"

I nodded.

"My father was a lamplighter. I remember every now and then he would come home with these beautiful insects – moths, butterflies, all sorts. These creatures would find their way over in all the strange cargoes and crates that would turn up at the docks."

"Our docks?"

Mr Munro nodded.

"Poor things would flit and flutter about the streets, not used to the dark and the cold, and as soon as the lamps were lit, there they would be, pushing against the glass to get to the light and the warmth. Most of them wouldn't last too long. My father would scoop them up and sell them on to the museum or collectors. I thought they looked so beautiful."

"You wanted to see the insects?"

"Maybe," said Mr Munro. "Don't see so many now there's not as many ships coming in."

"Perhaps I could be a lamplighter," I said, not really sure if I meant it or not.

Mr Munro smiled.

"Not long left for gas lamps; it's all going electric. No need for the likes of me. It'll be all clean light and wires, crackling and sparking all the time."

Mr Munro made sure that I was home safely. And then I watched from my window as he walked back down into the close across the street.

That night, I waited. Again, the lamplighter stood in the shadows, head bowed. It was not long until another figure approached. This time, the person hopped and bounced and I could see that it was a boy a little younger than myself. He seemed to know Mr Munro and stood by him, as if trying to engage him in a game. The lamplighter barely acknowledged him, but for one gesture, which was to point down into the close. Mr Munro was well known as a kind man, and he was especially good natured with children, so this strange behaviour unsettled and upset me. Mr Munro pointed one final time towards the close, then gathered his tools and walked off down the street. I watched as the boy stood, unsure, deciding what to do. After a moment, he turned and walked into the close.

At that moment, I resolved to do what the lamplighter should have done, and provide shelter and companionship to the lost boy. I slipped out of my house as quietly as I could, and ran down the stairs of our cold tenement and out across the street into the close.

The boy was standing at the far corner, where the tenement walls met. There was a glow there, which I took to be embers from a dying fire. He had his back to me, so, not wishing to startle him, I called out to him in a whisper.

At first it seemed that he had not heard me, and I was about to call out again. And then he turned. His motion was now slow and awkward, like a rusted wheel, grinding as it turns. As he finally faced me, I saw that I had made a terrible mistake. Two empty black eyes stared out from the boy's pale face, and his skin and features had slipped like melted candle wax. As he saw me, his misshapen mouth opened in a hideous silent scream, and, arms now outstretched, he ran towards me at great speed. I turned to flee and ran straight into Mr Munro. I panicked, turning back again to look at the boy, who was now standing still once more. Mr Munro patted my shoulders and gestured that I should stand behind him. He did not say a word, but instead pointed towards the corner. The boy took a tiny step towards him, but the lamplighter shook his head and kept pointing. Slowly, sadly, the boy turned and walked back towards the corner. Mr Munro turned now too, and gently pushed me back along the close. A bright light now shone behind us, growing brighter with every step back towards the street. And then it stopped, and the close and the street were once again in darkness.

"What was that?" I asked.

"It's not for us to see," said Mr Munro. "That's an end of it."

"But... the boy..."

Mr Munro nodded.

"There's lots of reasons people don't like the night-time, but some people are scared because they see what hides there," he said, looking at me, smiling sadly. "Is that not right?"

I thought of the grey faces I would see reflected in windows, of the figures who would stand behind me in mirrors, and of their always outstretched hands, thin and grasping.

"You see them too?" I asked. "Who are they?"

"People. Just people. Poor things. Lost in the cold, trying to stay where it's warm. And it's cruel to keep them here, circling around that light. Better to help them pass on into the dark."

"Down the close?"

"That close, the old railway by the berry yards, a tunnel beneath the docks... there's always places that seem to take you one way but lead you another."

"But..."

"Not for the likes of me to understand," said Mr Munro. "I just light the lamps. And switch them off too when that's what's needed. If I were you, I'd make your peace with the dark and all that's in it."

The lamplighter walked me back to my front door and was kind enough never to tell my mother about my misadventures.

After that, the lights on our street were kept on. Mr Munro guided his moths elsewhere. I think about him often, about his unquestioning sense of responsibility to something he could not understand or explain.

Over the next few years, the new electric lights flickered on all across the town. There was light. Light such as never before. Mr Munro himself passed on not so long after.

It was a cleaner light – colder, but bright enough to make the streets seem safer than they had ever been. So it seemed to everyone else.

But I see them all, trapped and flickering, throwing themselves endlessly towards our new light, and smashing up against it. There are not enough shadows to fall into, not enough old ways to wander into the dark.

Some seem to know that I see them and they follow me, waiting for me to reach out, to help, or to walk with them into the darkness. That same darkness I've run from my whole life.

There is no rest; those faces that once moved only amongst the night-time shadows now stare at me at every hour of the day, as if pleading with me to gather them up in the warmth of the living, or to usher them forever into the dark.

But I am no lamplighter.

THE BEAN-NIGHE OF GLEN AROS

Anna Cheung

In the dark of the night, over the trees of Glen Aros
a cry coiled from the forest, strangling roots,
like a serpent ensnared in the woodland web.

Aldith laid on her bed, eyelids heavy in dream,
hair latticed across rose-tinted cheeks,
pale yet feverish in a fitful sleep.

The sound slithered into the shadows
through creaky windows and splintered doors,
poisonous and sinewy in the deadly silence.

The cry was half human, half creature
and dragged Aldith from the arms of slumber.
She stumbled barefoot onto the stone-cold floor.

The Bean-Nighe of Glen Aros

She wandered, weary, into the woodland,
the thorns, pines and nettles snagging flesh,
but, finally, she found her way to the water's edge.

There, bent over by the brook, she saw
a woman, as gnarled and crooked as ancient trees.
Her claw-like feet clung onto the lichen rocks

as she scrubbed a pile of blood-stained rags.
Closer and closer Aldith creeped, but, alas,
the old hag had already foreseen!

With one eye, the creature honed in on the girl,
and spat, snaggle-toothed, into the brook.
Aldith recoiled at the sight of the crone.

I am a Seer, messenger from the Otherworld.
Come near and knowledge I will impart to your heart's desire.
Curious, the girl stepped closer and asked for her name.

Some call me Ban-sìth, some call me Lavandière.
I am Bean-Nighe, the midnight washerwoman.
Why be feart of me? Come hither, and I shall tell you more.

Aldith inched forward; the rocks were slippery-sleek.
I wash the clothes of mortals soon to drift
on their underworld journey to Death's Abyss. Come look!

Upon hearing those words, the girl's heart lurched –
there, against the hag's saggy breast clutched, she saw
her own frock, sodden on rocks and blotched with blood.

She staggered and fell into the water.

SOULMATES

Gavin Inglis

He was sitting in Greyfriars Kirkyard at sunrise, watching mud creep up the cover of Descartes' *Passions of the Soul* and wondering if it would be too much of a cliché to throw himself off North Bridge. She came past in clumpy boots and a velvet skirt, took her headphones out and yelled at him for letting a library book get stained. After that they were friends.

Turned out she was in the year above him in philosophy class and he was just a bit blocked on the separation of soul and body. She took him through a chemical argument against free will, told him to draw the six principal passions on paper like the colour wheel in art, and then he got it.

They started hanging out together. He made her a mixtape of the Cramps and she took him to the Monday Club and one night they crashed together in his single bed and sort of ended up kissing. It went further and in the morning they both blinked at the mirror with panda eyes and decided it hadn't spoiled anything and after that they were officially in a relationship.

They stuck with the goth scene for years, moving from group to group, keeping separate friends so they never became one of those trophy couples who wore matching outfits, sickened everybody and broke up after six weeks. Then club politics and the bitching got too much and they stopped going out, and moved in together. They didn't weed out the duplicates from their music collection but he did CDs and she preferred vinyl anyway.

It was only a few months before domestic bliss got boring and they realised they needed some other outlet besides the weekly late-night horror movie run. So, they took eight cans of Strongbow and a half bottle of blackcurrant cordial back down to Greyfriars, where they sat on a wall and got quietly smashed. A couple came by and the woman had the guy's trousers half down, right in front of them, before she noticed the black-clad figures perched in the shadows and shrieked. The guy went after her, trying to run and pull up his trousers at the same time. They finished their booze, put the empties in a bag to keep the graveyard clean, and afterwards agreed it had been their best night out in six months.

So, they started doing it properly. They went to Armstrong's and sorted out full Victorian outfits. He got a frock coat, top hat, a wing-collared shirt and a waistcoat that was cheap because moths had snacked on it. With a little corset work she got into full mourning, with a veil and a lace-edged parasol handmade in Chichester.

He splashed out for some decent white face paint and she showed him how to set it with powder. They slipped into the kirkyard after dusk and spent their time checking visibility and setting up ghostly moves. It took three nights before they had the choreography nailed: the synchronised turn and the unhurried drift behind one of the high walls.

Tour groups were great, on their way back from the Covenanters' Prison and the attentions of the Mackenzie poltergeist. Some screamed. Some ran. They were pretty sure a couple of teenagers wet themselves. The guides recognised the resident ghosts, of course; the office was right beside the gate and the couple went in and out in civvies. But they provided an extra attraction, asking for nothing in return. So, the tour company kept their secret.

At first they hid in a sepulchre or tomb; later, he found a viable exit over the west wall and she practised until she could mount the ledge in heels and full skirt. Not many people followed them anyway, but those times were the best, listening to groups freak out when they came through and found the West Yard deserted. Some early mornings, just to mix it up, they gazed through the George Heriot's gate at half-asleep schoolkids arriving for rugby or hockey trips.

Over time they wound it down: every couple of weeks, then once a month. Often she felt too tired. They tried it one night in the winding closes of the Royal Mile, but the yuppie bistros and tartan shops seemed to take the romance out of it. So, they saved their act for special occasions.

Three or four times he suggested the trip and she couldn't face it. Then a couple of other things happened and she got the blood tests and there it was on the paper: Adult Acute Lymphoblastic Leukemia. They talked about starting chemo immediately, but they took more samples and it was in her spine, in her brain. The doctors were kind, told her to go home, and they had a few more sunny weekends together and then, one morning, she was gone.

He didn't go out for a few days, and when he did, it was to ask about a plot in Greyfriars Kirkyard. The minister was very gentle but explained there were no new burials in the yard. If it would be a comfort, he could scatter her ashes there, on the consecrated ground. The funeral was a family affair, not very goth, and he got the plastic container the next day, surprised how heavy it was in his hands.

Weeks passed, a long sequence of nights and harsh sunlight, and her ashes sat in a cupboard until the moment felt right. Then he showered, moisturised and applied and set the face paint, like she had taught him. He pulled on the shirt, its collar looser than he remembered, donned the frock coat and settled the top hat on his head. It was 4.30am. He slipped through the deserted streets, scaled the wall and walked the familiar paths, leaving a little of her behind with every step.

In the following weeks, he was there every night, a solitary figure lingering by the gate or searching for something in the shadow of a tomb. The tour groups shrieked a little louder, and ran a little faster, at the hollow expression on that pale, shrouded face. Few followed him now, and even the tour guides hurried away to their shuttered office.

Then, one night, she was standing beside him again.

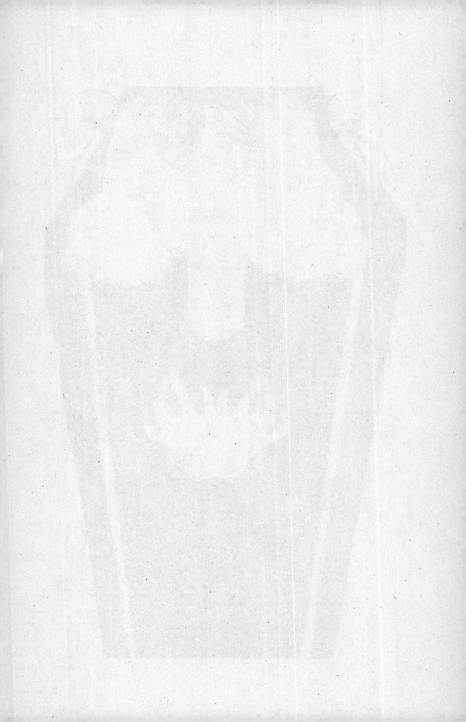

TWICE-BURIED MARY

Pauline Cordiner

Many years ago, in the village of Inverurie, there lived a young lassie named Mary Elphinstone. Now, Mary was as beautiful as she was kind and there were many suitors for her hand in marriage, but none had taken her fancy. None, that is, until the day that the new minister stepped up in front of his congregation to take his first sermon. Being a well-off family in the area, Mary's family were right up at the front of the kirk, and the minute he set his eyes upon her his mind was off his sermon and his heart was stolen by her smile.

To cut a long story short, it was no time at all until the two were courting and within the year they were married. There was no fine a couple as Mary and her Johnny. Now, I'm sad to say I'm going to ruin this romantic tale for you, for Mary soon became ill. She fell into unconsciousness and, one night, with Johnny holding her hand and weeping, she just slipped away.

Her husband was absolutely distraught. He couldn't think of a life ahead without his beloved Mary. He was so upset that, after the funeral, he couldn't even bear to go to his wife's wake, let alone stay with her body for the next few nights.

For, you see, this story takes place at a time when the Resurrection Men were hard at work in Scotland's graveyards. The Anatomy Act of 1832 was far in the future and the doctors and students of Aberdeen's anatomy schools needed bodies to dissect. With a limit of two hanged men per year for each district, grave robbing was a simple yet ghoulish solution. Families would watch over the graves of their loved ones – or employ mortsafes or mort-houses – until the body mouldering in the grave would no longer be fresh enough for the students to analyse.

Johnny was so swept up in his grief that poor Mary's body lay alone in her grave. Unguarded.

The local inn that night was busy, with many wishing to raise a glass or two to Mary's memory. *How tragic to die so young! And her poor husband! He won't leave the house, you know. Too upset to come to her wake or to stay by her body!*

Now, let us picture a couple of dark characters sitting in the corner of the inn drinking their ale. History doesn't tell us their names, so let's call them Big Jimmy and Wee Jimmy. They aren't grave robbers really – just opportunists. They're a bit down on their luck. They've been out of work for a while and have spent the whole day casing houses that seem easy to rob. Just imagine their ears pricking up at this! Poor Mary Elphinstone, buried just today in her wedding finery? And no one to guard her grave?

Well, the two of them nodded at each other, downed their drinks and left the inn. In the silence of the night, they wrapped sacking around the hooves and wheels of their horse and cart and quietly made their way through the streets to the graveyard. By now the moon was up and there was just enough light to see Mary's newly dug grave. Shovels were taken from the back of the cart and they began to dig. Well, it wasn't long before they reached the coffin, broke open the lid – and there she lay. They stared for a brief moment at Mary, buried in her wedding gown. But the silence was broken when Wee Jimmy spied the big shining red ruby ring on her finger.

"Will ye tak a look at that! Just imagine fu much money we can get fur that! We'll eat like kings for a month!" he said, reaching out and pulling on the ring.

Well, he rugged and he tugged, but it just wouldn't move.

"Haud on there," whispered Big Jimmy, and off he went to the cart, where he found a small handsaw. Surely the anatomists wouldn't take much off the price for a missing finger?

"If we can't haul the ring off, we can cut it aff just as easily!" said Big Jimmy, eyes gleaming.

Unfortunately for the robbers, but luckily for Mary, she wasn't actually dead – she had been buried alive! She had merely slipped into a coma, her heartbeat and breathing too shallow for the doctors of the day to detect. This whole time, her body had been recovering from her illness and healing itself – it was only a matter of time until she would awake.

When the saw started to cut through her flesh, the pain brought her quickly to consciousness. The sharp smell of decay and the sound of a man's haggard breath confused her. She opened her eyes and tried to make sense of the situation. In the moonlight she made out the distant shapes of the gravestones, the pile of earth lying next to her, the spade and crowbar lying beside, and the men above her so intent in their work that they had not noticed her awake.

It seemed to take an eternity to take a full breath, and it pained her lungs to do so, but fear had now taken hold, and so Mary let out such a bloodcurdling scream that the two Jimmys would remember it for the rest of their lives. Well, they dropped their tools and ran out of the graveyard, out of Inverurie and out of this story. Hopefully to start afresh – living good, honest lives. History does not tell us what happened to them next. But what about Mary?

Mary got to her feet and stood for a moment, shivering, barefoot in the soil, taking in the situation. Seeing no other alternative, she started the walk back through the streets to her home and her beloved Johnny. She glanced at the warm light coming from the windows of the inn as she went by, never guessing that the people inside were attending her wake.

In his grief, Johnny had locked the door to the manse, intent on drowning his sorrows, and had passed out in front of the cold hearth.

A frantic knocking at the door woke him from his sleep and he shook his head, muttering: "If I hidnae jist buried my beloved Mary, I'd swear that was her chappin at the door!"

He put it down to the drink and the upset and tried to go back to sleep in his armchair. But the knocking continued. Eventually he dragged himself to his feet and went to answer the door.

Well! Imagine his shock when he opened the door to find Mary standing there in the moonlight – pale as pale could be, with her feet black from the mud, and bedraggled hair, reaching out towards him with her bloodied hand.

"Oh, ma Johnny! I've come back tae ye!"

Imagining it was her spirit returned from the grave to haunt him, he fainted from the shock. When he came round, she was sobbing, mopping his brow and swearing they would never be apart again.

Mary returned to full health. They went on to have a fine family and live a long and healthy life. It is said that when death finally came they were still so much in love that they died within a few days of each other. And where were they buried? Well, it was back in the same lair which Mary had found herself in all those years before, earning her the name Twice-Buried Mary.

Now, the locals will tell you that if you visit Mary's grave today, and put your ear to the stone, you might just hear knocking...

But I think that's another story.

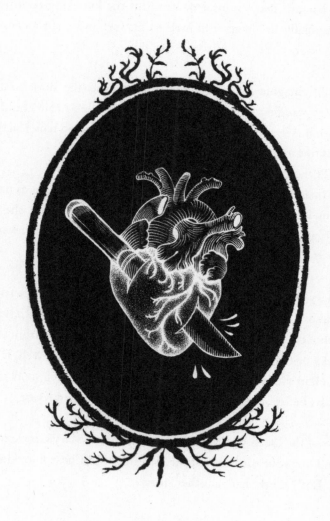

A GRAVEYARD WAGER

Duncan Williamson

I'll tell you a wee ghost story. Now, this is supposed to have really happened.

Once upon a time, and a long, long while ago in Argyllshire, och, many hundred years ago, when there was nae roads, nae pubs and nae nothing, and no many houses or nothing, and there was an odd inn house here or there along the track. You see?

Well, the country villagers, whoever they were, maybe crofters or farmers or shepherds, they used to always gather on a Saturday night in the inn. It being a big thing like a barn, you ken, where they selt beer and ale, and they would tell stories and say cracks and sing songs, you know, like an old-fashioned ceilidh? Well, this is hundreds of years ago. One would tell a story, one would sing a song, one would do this, one would do that, maybe perform an act or say poetry or that, just for the sake of having a good night, you see? Then they would all yoke their horses and go, by whatever means they could get, home to their own places.

Everybody had packed up for the night, and there was nobody left but three men and a woman. And they were sitting at this table and they were drinking. And the story got around about ghosts. One was telling one story about ghosts, one was telling another story about ghosts. But this lassie sitting at this table, she said, "There's nae such a thing as ghosts. I dinny believe in no ghosts."

"Well," says the inn owner. He says, "I believe in ghosts. And I'll tell you, lassie, what we'll do." He said, "You come here tomorrow night. Up there by my inn is the graveyard, where the folk's been getting buried for the last two hundred years." And he says, "It's haunted."

The lassie says, "It's no haunted. I don't believe in hauntings."

"Well," he says, "I'll tell you what we'll do," he says. "There's these three men here and you," he says, "and me. Tomorrow, you come down here. The whole lot of yous. And we'll go up to the graveyard. We'll stick a knife in the graveyard. We'll stick a knife in a grave." And he said, "Tomorrow night is Saturday night. You come here, and go up there at twelve o'clock, and bring back that knife, and I'll give you five pound and a full bottle of whisky" – now, in these days it was a *lot* of money – "if you can do that."

"I'll do it," says the young lassie. "I'll do it. I'm no feart of nae ghosts. Nae ghosts will bother me."

"*I* wouldny do it," said the men. "No for a bet or a wager would I go to a graveyard for – no – nothing under the sun," says the men.

She says, "I'll go."

"Well," says the inn owner to the men, "if you're game?"

"Oh," says the men – three young men – "we'll come down tomorrow. The morn's Saturday and we're no doing very much."

So, the next day was Saturday and the three young men made their way down to the inn. And they met the inn owner. And the young lassie was there. So, the five of them walked up to the graveyard. And, as he was leaving, the inn owner just walked into the kitchen and took a kitchen knife in his hand. And he walked up and he stuck the kitchen knife into a grave.

Well, round a grave – if you've ever seen it yourself, if you've been to a graveyard – a set of railings, round the grave? Have you ever seen a set of old iron rails?

"Right," says the inn owner. "Now, you come up the night," he says, "and pick up that knife." And he says, "Fetch it back through that rail," he says, "while we're there in the pub. And you'll get your five pound," he says, "and a bottle of whisky." Well, it was five old guineas in them days, or five silvers or whatever it was. Anyway, the lassie says, "Alright."

So, they drank away and they crack and tell stories, till the same thing happened the next night: there was no one left but the three young men, the inn owner and the lassie.

The lassie whaps her coat about her, ties her hanky on her head and away she goes. Walks up to the graveyard.

The men sits and they sits and they sits and they sits...

But no. There was no sign of the lassie coming back.

They sit till daylight, till six o'clock, till it got clear.

She never turned up.

So, they went to the inn owner and they telt him. They says, "That lassie never come back."

"Ah," says the inn owner, "well, she did it for a wager."

"Well," says one of the three young men, "it's clear now. There's nothing to bother us. Come on with me," he said, "the three of us."

"I'll go with you," says the inn owner. He says, "I'll go with you too."

So, the four of them walked up to the graveyard. And there, at the grave, was the lassie.

She had the knife in her hand. And she was lying in the wee path — a wee path that was worn with folk walking past — and she was lying dead.

So, they wondered what had really happened. And I'm going to tell you what really happened.

The lassie left the inn, and she walked up to the grave. And, in these days, they wore big long swishy coats, you ken, big long dresses. She wasny feart. So, she leaned over to the grave and she picked up the knife. And she whirled round to get awa. And when she whirled round, didn't the tail of her coat catch on the railings? And as she walked awa she felt something *gripping* her.

See what I mean? When she whirled around, her frock caught on the spike of the railings, on one of the spikes, and as she walked awa she felt the thing pulling her back. And, with the fright she got, she drappit down dead.

That's right. She drappit down dead with the fright.

So, the three men and the inn owner walked back. And that's what the man says: "Never again," he said, "in this inn," he said, "as long as I'm here," he said, "will ever I wager for money." And until his dying day he never did.

And that's what really happened.

So, that's a ghost story for you. And that was true. That was a true story.

I heard that from old Julie McDonald years and years and years ago. An old storyteller. Telt me that crack. Was supposed to have happened up in Argyllshire.

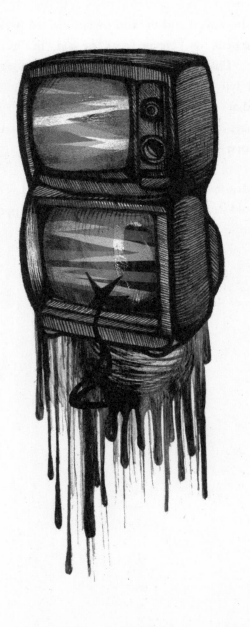

SCAN LINES

Ali Maloney

Now that no one plays VHS anymore, I never see my dad.

For a long time, I only saw him when I went to the video shop. In the back room, where all the unrated videos with colourful and lurid covers gathered dust, was a beat-up TV. The new owners of the shop didn't mind me going back there, even though it was supposed to be for over-18s only. They knew that I wasn't looking at the pornographic covers or twisting my mind round the violent blurbs; I'd come to see my dad.

I'd turn the TV on – sometimes you had to hold the 'on' button down or it would switch itself off – and press 'play' on the in-built VCR. It always smelled like burning dust and rotten eggs as it whirred and screeched into life. The video in the player – there was only that one as the 'eject' button was broken – had originally been a trailer reel for forthcoming attractions, but was now so worn and thin that the original footage was almost completely indistinguishable. Amongst the fizzle and static and scan lines, I could see my reflection in the screen; I'd see my dad standing in the doorway behind me, looking over my shoulder.

I'd go there every day after school. I was normally the only one there, apart from the owner sat behind his counter fiddling with his Game Boy, of course – and my dad.

He'd never say anything, but he didn't need to. I knew what he would say; he wouldn't approve that I was wasting my afternoon in a video store when I could be out playing football or climbing trees. He never understood.

I had tried to speak to him before, but he didn't move, didn't answer. The only reply I ever got was a shout from the front room: "You talking to me?"

So, we didn't speak.

I just hung out with my dad in the back of the video store.

One day, I turned up and all the lights were off. The video store was closed. I tried to peer through the windows to see if my dad was waiting for me, but the door to the back room was closed.

The next day, after school, I went again. This time the shelves were all empty. There was still no one there.

On the last day, the sign was gone, and a sepia poster promised that an artisanal coffee shop and bakery was coming soon. There was a skip outside piled high with all the shop fittings and videos. I climbed in. I wasn't interested in the videos, although I wondered why they would throw them out rather than try to sell them. There was only one thing I was trying to find.

I found it at the bottom of the skip, smashed. I tried to gather the shards and circuits and broken glass. The pieces snapped and unspooled in my arms. I couldn't even tell what was VCR and what was the cabling ripped from inside the plaster walls.

It was beyond repair; I'd never see my dad again.

Years later, after I had left school and left town, I happened to be driving past and saw that the coffee shop was still there. Still in business after all these years. I stopped in for an Americano and started chatting to the guy behind the counter. I told him that there used to be a video store here. He told me that he knew, that he had bought the place from them. I asked what had happened. "No one wants videos anymore," he said. "Dead medium," he said. "Besides," he said, "the place was haunted."

THE GIRL IN THE SAUNA

Daiva Ivanauskaitė

Spell: Svidu, žibu, tvasku, skaistinuosi…

Every summer, with my Scottish family, I go to the Isle of
Bute. And, standing on Ettrick Bay beach, I always remember
a time on a wild beach at the Baltic Sea, near the Lithuanian
and Latvian border. It was a cloudy day with drizzle, too cold
to swim. I was with friends and we built our own sauna. We
made a big bonfire and heated up huge rocks in it. Then we
used wooden poles to create the tent structure and covered it
with polytunnel material. We put our swimming suits on and
gathered inside the self-built sauna around the steaming stones.
When our bodies were warm enough, we ran outside and
submerged ourselves in the cold waves of the sea.

Living in Scotland, I miss my wonderful little country, Lithuania. One thing that I really miss is a good natural wooden
smoke sauna, which we in Lithuanian call a pirtis. A traditional
pirtis is a little wooden hut all covered in black smoke stains. It's
an edgy-looking place, usually next to a river, a pond or a lake,

with smoke coming out the chimney or sometimes just out the window and door. A pirtis is a magical place where all creative elements – fire, water, earth and air – meet. It's a place where transformation has a very clear expression through washing, bathing, purifying and leaving the old skin behind, especially with the help of rituals of hot salt, honey, leafy whisks made out of oak or birch or linden tree branches, and jumping into icy water to cool down.

After a good pirtis, it's not only the body that feels new: the head starts emptying of worries. As this is the place where different worlds meet, it is no surprise that you can meet Dievas (God), dangerous laumės (fairies) or the cheeky trickster Velnias (the devil).

Everyone knows it is a very bad idea to stay alone in a pirtis late at night.

Once, in a small village, there was a family: a husband and wife and their two daughters. It was not a perfect family. For some reason, the wife preferred one daughter over the other, Marytė. One Saturday night, she told Marytė to wait and have her pirtis separately, after she and Marytė's sister finished their bathing, as the pirtis was now too small for the three of them. Marytė waited for her turn, as she was told, and finally came to the pirtis very late at night. She undressed, stepped into the hot steaming room, sat on a wooden bench, and was about to relax when…

Knock.

Knock.

Knock.

She heard the knocking at the door and the pleasant voice of a young man.

"Good evening, pretty girl! Step outside and join me for a dance!"

Marytė immediately understood who the young man was. Her heart started to beat faster. At last, she replied.

"Oh, good evening, young man! That is so kind of you! I would love to join you for a dance. But you see, I just started my bath. I am looking around and I see that there is no soap left. I can't join you, being unwashed."

But the young lad was, as you guessed, the Devil, so, with a blink of an eye, soap made out of honey appeared in her hands.

Well, Marytė took her time having a good wash. But *knock knock knock.* The young man was impatient.

"My lovely, are you washed? Are you finished? Step outside and let's head to the dance."

"Well, I'm afraid I can't step outside, as I am all dripping wet. And there is no towel left for me."

And, with a snap of the fingers, the whitest and softest towel appeared on the shoulders of Marytė.

The girl took her time drying herself very, very thoroughly.

The man was knocking again.

"Come on! Now you should be all ready to dance."

"Well, actually, I see a problem here. For a dance I do not have a dress."

And, with a wink of an eye, Marytė realised that she was wearing a beautiful dress with dainty silver embroidery! She looked magnificent!

The gentleman outside was very eager now.

"Oh, show up! I want to look at you! With this dress you are all set to go to the dancing party!"

"Yes, this dress is breathtaking! I have never seen anything like this before! But I think it's not a good idea to dance barefoot."

And there you go. A couple of new shiny shoes appeared on her feet.

The young man was now very desperate.

"Oh, come! Come outside and let's go! We've already missed the beginning of the party."

"Oh, that's unfortunate. But I need a brush for my long hair."

And one, two, three: Marytė holds a silver hairbrush.

"Well, are you ready?"

"Not yet! I need a mirror! I can't see what I'm doing."

And oplia! A golden mirror in Marytė's hand.

She brushed her hair slowly and meticulously.

The Devil lost his temper. The knocking became very intense.

"Oh, my star! You *must* be a doll now! Step outside and let's hurry up if we want to enjoy the last dance!"

"I am almost ready! I just need some hairpins."

"Oh, my goodness. Here you go. A devil's dozen of pins should be enough. All made out of pearls."

Marytė, one by one, picked up the pins and slid them into

her hair, pinning her strands into a nice hairdo. And now she was ready.

But, as she slid in her last hairpin, the cockrel sang its song. Marytė opened the door and stepped outside, but…

The Devil was gone.

At dawn she returned home all dressed up like a queen.

The mother and sister could not believe their eyes. Marytė had to tell the whole story. So, the next week, on Saturday night, Marytė's sister was left alone in the pirtis after everyone had had a bath. And, just after midnight, she heard the knocking, and a sweet male voice inviting her to dance.

Well, this girl was ready and prepared for this moment, so she listed all the things she wanted at once – soap, towel, dress, pair of shoes, mirror, hairbrush, hairpins – and she added a few extra things on top.

Well, with the wink of an eye, with a snap of the fingers, all the things she wanted appeared in front of her at once!

The next morning, this girl did not return home.

The family went down to the pirtis.

It was empty, the door wide open.

No one had seen her.

No one had heard a thing.

She was lost forever.

THE FIRE AND THE FACTOR

Jeannie Robertson

Did ever you hear the one about Silly Jack and his mother when he murdered the factor – not for the money but just because he hadn't the sense? I'll tell you that one.

I didn't hear my grandfather telling this one, it was my mother I heard telling it.

You see, there was an old woman and she had a little wee croftie placie. And she had one son, and they called him Jack. He was really right off. But she idolised him just the same – it was all the company that she had. Of course, she did all the work about the place. They were very, very poor. It just took them to keep theirselves.

One day she was going awa from home and she said, "Now, Jack," she says, "I'm going awa from home the day, but I'll maybe be back in time before the factor gings awa. He'll be in by here maybe in the afternoon some time. Have on a big peat fire so that the factor will get a good heat while he's sitting waiting upon me. Because he'll maybe be here before I come back. And you'll mind and put on a good fire."

And he says, "Aye, mother. I'll put on a good peat fire," he says, "and I'll have the fire ready for the factor coming in fast."

"Ah, well," she says, "laddie, that's what to do. I winna be awfa long."

Awa his mother gings anyway.

She'd been away an hour or two when in by comes the factor looking for his six-monthly rent, you see?

The factor says, "Your mother in, Jack?"

"Nah, nah," he says, "my mother's awa the day. But she telt me to tell you to sit down and take a rest and you'll get a heat and she maybe winna be awfa long. She didna want you to gang awa," he says, "until she comes back, and you'll get your money."

"Oh, well," he says, "Jack, I'll sit down and I'll take a rest, of course."

The factor sits down upon the chair in front of this big peat fire – it was a very cold day – and he made hisself as comfortable as he possibly could. But with the heat of this fire, the factor falls asleep.

Poor Jack, he was sitting at the other side of the fire, trying to make *his*self as comfortable as he could, until his mother would come in. And he's sitting watching the factor. And the factor fell sound asleep with the heat of the fire. And Jack's sitting looking into his face.

Suddenly, there's a great big fly lighted on the factor's brow, his baldy brow. And Jack got fascinated by this fly, travelling back and forward right over the factor's baldy head, and upon his brow.

He watched it for a good while. But, being no very right, god help us, he couldna help hisself and he says, "Come off the laird's brow, man!"

But, of course, the fly didna come off.

He waits for a wee while. This fly's still running about on top of the factor's baldy head and his baldy brow. So, he says, "Come off the laird's brow, man!"

But this fly is still sitting on his brow.

Jack sits for a while longer and he watches it.

He's beginning to get a wee bittie agitated now by this fly. So, he says, "Come off the laird's brow, man! Oh god, you bugger, you winna come off, will you?"

So, up gets poor Jack and he lifts the axe that he was awa hacking up all the sticks with, and he hits the fly, for to knock it off the laird's brow, but of course... He had the fly, right enough! But he killed the factor.

When his poor mother comes home, she gets the factor lying with his head hammered in two with the axe. She realised what her poor silly son had done. And she knew that this was one thing that he wouldna get off with. It'd be the means of taking her son awa from her and putting him in to some place. Well, naturally, him being all that she had, she was ready to put up a fight for to save her son.

They had a big goat – a big billy goat – and they cried it 'The Factor'. That was its name! So, Jack wasna very wise, but he wasna as silly as his mother made him out to be. She thought things right over. There was only one way to save her son. To make him look worse that what he was. Really make things look as if he was all muddled.

They took the factor and they buried him, him and her. But she kent that he would tell the police when they came round questioning about the factor, you see? She kent that he would tell the police.

So, she killed the billy goat, and she took the factor out of the grave, that him and her buried him into, and she put the billy goat into the same grave, you see? And she went away further and built a new grave and buried the factor herself in the new grave. You see? Without Jack's help.

She went up the lum and she telt him to look up the lum. But before she went up the lum she made a pot of porridge and milk, you see? She telt him, "Look up the lum!" When he looked up the lum, she poured down the pot of cold porridge and milk. And as it was coming down the lum, the poor fool was gobbling it up. She telt him, "It's raining porridge and milk!" And he thought it, with it coming down the lum.

So, whatever, any way or another, a while passed, and the police are going around all the houses and making enquiries to everybody. Did they see the factor? When had they seen him last and what time? What hour? So, of course, they come to Jack and his mother. They asked her and she telt them what time she saw him at. But of course, remember, she hid the bag with the money. So, whatever, any way or another, the police questioned them upside down and backside foremost. And poor silly Jack, he says, "Aye, man," he says, "I killed the factor."

His mother kent that he would say that, you see – he would tell the truth.

"Oh, you killed the factor?" the police says. "And where did you put him?"

"God, man!" he says. "Me and my mother buried him up here! Come on," he says, "and I'll let you see where I buried the factor."

The police went up with him, for to see where he had buried the factor, and his mother came up with them.

"My god," she said, "would you mind that poor silly laddie?" she says. "He doesna ken what he's speaking about." She says, "It's no right. You shouldna be questioning him. He'll say aye to everything. But, of course," she says, "you can dig up the grave. But you'll get a surprise."

"No, hold your tongue now, mother! *I* killed the factor," he says. "And me and you buried him in here."

"Well, well," she says, "it's all right. What next? When *did* you kill the factor?"

"God, mother," he says, "I mind fine," he says. "It was yon day it was raining porridge and milk."

"Oh, god bless me," the policeman says, "and this man. He's far from being right," he says, when he heard him saying it was raining porridge and milk. "But, nevertheless," he says, "we'll have to dig up this grave. He insists that he killed the factor, so we'll have to dig up the grave."

So, they come to a new grave. Of course, the lads start to dig, and they dug up the grave. They did dig out the thing that was buried in the grave. And when they pulled it out, this was the billy goat. It had horns, you see? So, as they were pulling it out, the poor fool looked down at the top of the thing that they were pulling out of the grave. He was expecting to see the dead man, but when he saw the billy goat coming out, he said, "Good god almighty, mother! He's grown horns and whiskers since we buried him here last!"

The police said, "Oh, god bless me. The poor laddie," he says, "you havena to mind him." And the case was dropped and the factor was never seen or heard tell of. And the whole thing was: the authorities thought that the factor had skedaddled awa with all the money and wasna to be gotten. And therefore it left poor Jack and his mother with all the money and him free of the murder and now left to bide with his poor old mother.

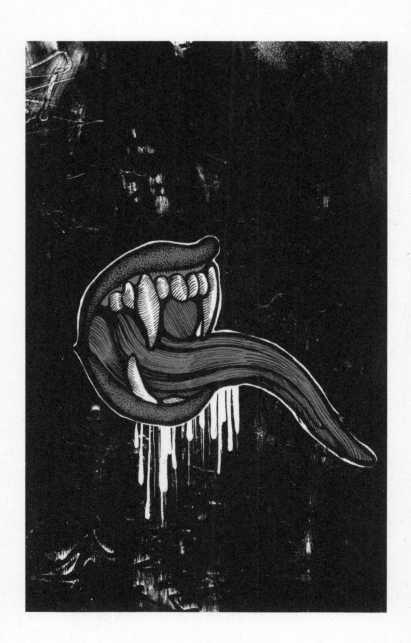

FROM ABYSS TO ABYSS

Paul McQuade

We don't eat tongues anymore. *You* don't, I mean. Sometimes it's easy to forget – that I am not one of you, that we are not you. That is the saddest thing about us. You see only the grisliness of our diet, how we survive the years so much longer than your kind. You do not understand the sadness we feel, being close but forever not quite a part of you. At some point, perhaps, we were of a species. One with each other. The single root of some great tree before some disaster sent us diverging. Those were the discoveries of the age in which I was born. The evolution of species, the great language of the Indus valley, the discovery of the germ, of lifeblood, the atom. Your age is not marked by great discoveries but a distortion of place in some new inter-connectedness I cannot bring myself to understand. Rather, it is the subtle changes I note: you do not eat tongue. Oh, some of you, yes, and your grandparents still. But the delectability of the organ is lost on you. Is this a symptom or a by-product? Does it signal a change? It is hard to tell what will take root among you. The smallest seed may find itself tangled in the warp of the century, while death and disease affect you not one bit. You are a mystery, even now, to me. And I find myself wondering what it means, this change in taste, though I suppose it is no surprise that someone like me – if I even am *someone* – should take an interest in the tongue. It is, after all, the key difference between us: you are born with a tongue, nestled in your tiny mouth, sleeping. The first language you speak is yours. You devour the language of your mother. We are not like you, in this regard. Unlike you, we cannot sustain ourselves in this most primary cannibalism. We cannot eat our mother's tongue.

When a wolf has young, the cubs claw dumbly on fur matted with blood and amniotic fluid until they find that aperture, that great opening onto life, from where they draw their mother's milk. So, too, did I, without sense, search mutely in the clotted earth of that Edinburgh graveyard in 1806, while the woman who brought me into this world pulled up her skirts and walked back to sell flowers. My mother left me pawing at the graves, the tombstones like closed doors, pushing at the earth until I finally found a grave that would yield to me. Down through the dirt, through the splintering wood of the coffin lid, into the shell of the skull. I cracked the jawbone open and drank, like an oyster, the rotten organ in the corpse's head. Mother's milk and mother tongue. These things you devour, when you are born. For us, the first tongue we eat is always a dead one.

And I was lucky. There are many whose first tongue is so far gone they begin life as crumpled, soiled things. Or simply stupid, a stupid life of stupid meals, barely better than animals. I, on the other hand, had the great fortune to come upon a man of means and education in that soft earth. A former minister of the kirk, barely dead a week, passing by a depression of the breath induced by laudanum. I could taste the ruby liquid on the tongue as I ate it. And as I devoured it, I felt the shape of myself come into being – a reconstitution, a mirroring of the man who had been, and whose remains lay in that rosewood box, which lay there, open to the night as if defiled by beasts.

Which is, of course, how they explained these mysterious coffin lids opening and closing in the night. Starving dogs – and not far off they were, too. Though Edinburgh is long inured to grave robbers. The good minister himself had a surgeon friend at the college who would take his students down to the graves for fresh specimens. With money, prestige and power, any eye could be turned. Plus ça change…

Yes, I was lucky. It was not a dullard I ate that night, nor some half-rotten thing. A fine upstanding man I became in that grave-yard. But, looking back, I think of that minister's life as strangely removed from the time he lived in. A head filled with medi-cine, politics, philosophy, but no real understanding of the lives around him, for all he had his own dark secrets. He walked in the shadows when it suited, yes. But for the most part he kept to the loftier circles, like lanterns facing each other across great depth. The kind of intellectual fire that avoids the mire of the abyss.

However detached the minister may have been, and for all that I had been pressed into his shape, with his memories and his language, I am – *we* are – driven, fundamentally, by hunger and by need. I could not enter society so easily bearing the likeness of a dead man. Such attempts by my kind are met, inevitably, with horror and with death. Fortunately, the minister's tongue, my first tongue, guided me that night. As much as the words it once spoke, that tongue held all the secrets it could not bear to give breath to in life. Great dams of the unsaid, pooling at the root.

So it was that I found myself in a public house in Newmarket. A few people recognised my face, certainly, as I came in. But no one here had been so close to the minister to have heard of his death just quite yet, it seemed. I leaned on the bar and waited, casting my eye across the crowd as casually as I could. A pub crew like any other, until you looked closely. Then you began to notice: there were no women, and the clothes the men wore were as likely to be of silk as of sackcloth. There were fine gentlemen and navvies and highlanders in their tartan wrap. A man drifted toward me from the crowd, one I had known before, or the minister had, at least. He smiled and held out a hand. I took it, greedily.

We did not speak. The relationship he and the minister had was not one based on words but on the forgetting of words, on the unfolding of pleasure in those dark alleys beyond the public and beyond rebuke. But as he led me down that darkness, did he sense it? The change in the flesh? That something was amiss? I do not know; his kiss was tentative, compared to the memories I had of him, those other man's memories. But the heat was the same. The living heat of blood. The soft glow of it like an open door in the cold. I closed my eyes and sought it out: his tongue, alive in my mouth. And I bit it. I bit down and the blood flowed sharp and coppery and I chewed the juices of that muscle until I felt myself begin, again, to change. A return to shapelessness. To the misery of being without form. But temporarily, thankfully. I was, once more, remade.

Abyssus ad abyssum invocat. These were the words I thought, coming into my new shape. The deep calls to the deep. The abyss is a place in the ocean, the darkest, most secret part. *Abyssus ad abyssum invocat.* A lovely phrase, learned from the minister. Psalm 42. I have clung to that psalm over the years: *As the hart cries with longing for the waters of the stream, so too does my soul cry with longing, to you, O God.*

I think of this psalm whenever I think of that first night. And whenever I think of the many things that came after. When I realise that I am condemned to destroy the things I wish to hold and love and cherish – that, like fire, I consume what is near to me like oxygen.

And so it has gone. For over two centuries now. This incessant hunger for a shape I will outgrow, forever haunted by the form of the last tongue I ingested. I have seen so much over the years, been so many people while never quite being a person. I have been a man, a woman, neither; have been young and old and back again. I have been what you call a monster, a title I have at times reviled and at others rejoiced in. Over the years I have found that, sometimes, it is far easier to be a monster than it is to be human. To be you. To be one of you. But of course, we are not – *I* am not – one of you.

What I am I am not quite sure. It is not in our nature to consider our existence so much as yours. This is inevitable. We are parasites. Our only way into this world is through you. This is true in the abyss of our very being. Your world is not our world, but we have no world of our own. And so I have lingered here, with you, as the tides have withdrawn, leaving the world so unrecognisable…

I have never thought to leave Edinburgh. Its streets change slowly, the shopfronts fade and renew, but the stonework is the same, the bones of the place. Perhaps it is this that makes the changes so palpable. Small changes, some – you don't eat tongue, for one. Others larger, if more intangible. It is as if the air itself has changed since the Age of Reason. I walk down the street today and there are words in the air. I taste so many tongues, in so many heads, moving at once in this globe you have fashioned with telephones and war. I see how this changes you. Your ears have become disused. You are forever looking at screens, at little panels of light. Such brief illumination. It is strange. To us, language must be eaten with the mouth, though this word is an injustice to the act. We do not simply eat: we incorporate, we embody, we become. But always with our mouths and teeth. This does not seem to be true for you. For you the eye is a mouth that stays forever wanting, as is the ear and the hand. Some part of you is always devouring. Every inch of you filled with some desire. And us? Our desire? For us, there is only one hunger. And it is also our curse: of being, forever, what we eat.

THE THING IN THE CORNER

Jude Reid

It was in the room again when I woke – the dark, shapeless terror that had visited me every night since I had returned from the Transvaal. I knew that I need only light the lamp to banish it, but found myself, as always, quite unable to extend my hand into the dark to do so. When at last the gas flared into life with a sooty plume, the room was empty again – empty of all but myself and the drowsing shape of my wife.

Isobel sat up and rubbed at her eyes. "The dream again?"

I nodded, stiff and mute.

"Come back to bed."

With tentative hands, she coaxed me down to my pillow. Her body was soft under her nightgown, but sleep and all other comforts had done with me for the night. Instead, I lay with the fear-sweat cooling on my skin, Isobel curled beside me in a spill of fiery hair, until the bedroom filled with grey light and I had no further need of the lamp.

There was no respite for me in sleep. Every night the same horror unfolded. I would find myself lying in darkness that was thick and absolute, my nose and mouth packed with dirt. That same soil pressed down on my chest, my throat and my helpless limbs. Each time my struggle back to wakefulness felt like a battle close fought and only narrowly won. And then there was the thing in the corner. Twisted, coiled and malevolent, it shrank away at the merest touch of the light. At first, I had thought it nothing but a remnant of my nightmare, conjured into the waking world by an overwrought imagination – but I soon learned that to continue in that hope was to abandon reason for self-delusion.

It seemed to me that I alone could perceive the thing. My wife was oblivious, and the household staff so bovine in their contentment that they could not possibly have sensed the horror that moved amongst us. I spent my days walking the grounds, preferring their thin autumn sunlight to the dingy rooms and passageways of Anstruther House. There were still shadows outside, of course, in the overgrown woodland paths and the chapel by the north wall, but with care I could avoid both on my routes. When the daylight faded I would retreat to the brightest rooms of the house, and place my trust in gaslight to keep the dark at bay.

As for my wife, it seemed that during my absence an afflic-tion had come over her, one that I was as powerless to explain as she was unwilling to acknowledge. At first, she was as loving as the bride I had left behind me. Her caresses were tender and yet somehow anxious, as though she feared that at any moment I might vanish. I told myself that this was not so unusual in a soldier's wife, especially one who had until so recently thought herself a widow – but her fluttering, moth-like concern grew until it intruded upon our every interaction.

After a time, I found myself wondering if this change in her had another cause – an event, perhaps, that had occurred while I was gone – and felt a glimmer of treacherous mistrust take root in my soul. Was my wife's unease related to the spectral presence of which she claimed to be unaware? Had some action of hers – betrayal, infidelity, an unfulfilled desire – conjured this shade into our lives? Though she was as meek and solicitous as ever, I began to detect in her the signs of a guilty conscience, and, beneath that, an unease that bordered on fear. My love for her became tainted first with suspicion and then with loathing.

When I could bear it no more, I confronted her and demanded to know the nature of the secret that had come between us.

"There is something in this house," I said. "Something that does not belong here."

Isobel bit her lip, and I knew my words had found their mark. She shook her head, lacking the strength to muster a lie. It seemed she had aged ten years in a moment, and those eyes, which had once gazed upon me with adoration, now held only fear and revulsion. In the corner of the room the shadows deepened.

"What have you done?" I asked her.

For a long moment she was silent, and then – haltingly at first – made her confession.

"They told me you were missing in action," she said. "First by telegram, and then a letter, hand-delivered by a little half-pay Captain who said you had been lost in the attempt to relieve Ladysmith. So many were dead, he told me – and though your body had not yet been found, he thought I should not hold out much hope for your return. If I should need help, he told me, I should not hesitate to call upon him." Her face twisted with disgust. "I knew already he was counting me a widow, and one to whom he intended to pay attention of the most unwelcome kind.

"When he left, I was angry that he was alive – that ridiculous little man with his leer and his moustache – when my own beloved husband was dead and rotting on the other side of the world. I drank too much that evening. Sherry, gin, brandy – anything I could find – but none of it was enough to make me forget. I ended the night stumbling around in the dark, driven half insane with sorrow and spirits, and not particularly caring what would become of me.

"And then, by chance – or so it seemed – I found myself in the old chapel by the north wall. I remembered standing there on our wedding day. I thought of all our hopes and plans, and how they had come to nothing. I think – I think madness came over me. I tore the cross from the wall, the cloth from the altar, and dashed them to the ground, screaming obscenities to the God who had abandoned me. Had I not worshipped? Had I not served and obeyed – only for the reward of an empty bed and a lifetime of fruitless sorrow?

"And when it was all over, and I was standing, disgusted by the wreckage of my faith, I saw the man in the corner of the room. He was old and dressed head to toe in black. He must have been witness to the whole affair. My face was burning with shame – I stammered apologies, insisting that I would never have behaved so had I known a living soul was there to see – but the man seemed more amused than horrified by my blasphemies. And he asked me that if, as it seemed, I was done with God, with whom would I be throwing my lot in now?

"It must have been that the drink made me bold, for I answered that if it would return you to me, I'd gladly kiss the feet of the Devil himself. I regretted the words as soon as they left my mouth – I blundered outside and emptied my guts of the night's excesses. When I returned, the old man was gone, and come morning I might have dreamed the whole affair, so unreal it seemed in the light of day.

"The empty weeks passed. And then another telegram arrived saying you had been found – frail, sick and much the worse for your time in Waterval – but alive and coming home to me! I gave thanks to God – I begged His forgiveness for my lack of faith, never once thinking your return might not be the miracle it seemed."

She closed her eyes. My hand hesitated in the air beside her face. I would have caressed her, had I not known that she would recoil from my touch.

"My husband died at Spion Kop," she said. "Something else came back to me."

Spion Kop. The name brought the memories in a gush, blood from an open wound. I remembered it all now – the white rasp of the bayonet between my ribs, the surprise on the Afrikaner's face as he heaved it free, the blur of sky and cloud as I fell. A snap at the base of my skull as a booted foot broke my neck, then panic as my lungs filled with a froth of churned earth and my own blood.

Nothing. And then, again, a sudden sense of being. Earth filling my mouth and nose as I dug mole-blind, drawn to the surface like a maggot to decay. The prickle of healing flesh, senses returning inch by painful inch, retching up blood-stained clods of earth. My lungs heaved and shrieked until at last they were empty of soil and I drew the agonising first breath of a second life.

I was shaking by the time I opened my eyes. Isobel was silent, hands pressed to her mouth, staring past me to the corner of the room. I turned, and there it was, that black shape all curled and twisted in on itself like an immolated corpse. It had no eyes, no nose to speak of, but the hunched back and gnarled hands might have been those of an old man. The mouth was wide in a leer of mockery and anticipation. I saw a flash of white teeth, and the curve of a long, red tongue.

I leaned forward and put my lips to Isobel's ear, so close I could feel the burning heat of her skin, close enough to kiss.

"Now do you see it?" I whispered.

THE PRIEST OF FORVIE

P. D. Brown

During that sweep of centuries called the Middle Ages, the villagers of Forvie, on the Aberdeenshire coast to the south of Collieston, lived a life bound to the rhythm of the seasons and the moods of the sea. Bound also were their lives, indeed their very souls, to the Church. The year and the sea both gave harvests in return for hard work. The Church gave comfort to troubled minds and the assurance of eternal life to worried souls – in return for tithes and absolute obedience.

Forvie's kirk, the only stone building in the village, had been built sometime during the twelfth century, on the site of an older chapel, possibly dating back to the seventh. In the year 1410, the sudden death of their then priest was a shock to them all, mainly because of the suddenness of his death but also because of the immediate lack of a spiritual father to whom any of them could turn, in whom any of them could confide their deepest secrets. The new priest when he arrived in due course was a shock of a different kind, for whilst the previous priest had been a plump and jolly yet sensitive man, the new priest was tall, thin and pale. His black hair matched the darkness of his eyes. These features, together with his long black robe, conspired to give the impression of some great dark bird – a cormorant, a raven or some other bird of ill omen. He certainly had an unearthly aura about him. He was chill of manner and stand-offish.

When he first arrived in the village, he went straight to his new lodgings and thence to the kirk, where he stayed the remainder of the day. The following day also he spent alone in the kirk. He never went to any of the villagers' houses to introduce himself. His only dealings with the villagers were those directly required by the performance of his ceremonial and other churchly duties.

It was at confession that he began to perturb his parishioners, for he would question them searchingly and thoroughly as to the motives for and the causes of their occasions of sin. This, then, was how the new priest chose to get to know his flock – by prising from them, in return for absolution, every grievance and resentment, every anger and anguish. No villager ever spoke to another about this; what was talked of in the confessional was not open to discussion. So, they all felt but did not yet share a growing unease, an unease that was compounded when, in the following weeks, he would sometimes say to a confessor what others had spoken to him from that same very seat. Such breach of confidence was shocking but they did not dare question a priest. Not unsurprisingly though, these little drops of poison, dropped in their ears, little drops of what others had really done, or said, or thought, began to congeal and fester, then rankle and anger.

Slowly, then, was dissension and distrust sown between friends and neighbours, between husband and wife, between parent and child. The harmony of village life was quite gone, for all were whispered about and all whispered gossip, which went round and round the village and beyond to the surrounding countryside. And, at the centre of it all, like a black maggot in a rotting apple, sat the priest of Forvie.

The priest himself did not escape the gossip. So often was he in the kirk alone, not just during the day but also, and more often, at night, when he would lock himself in, that the villagers began to believe that he was practising black magic and devilish arts in God's House. His housekeeper had told how the priest had several large books bound with lockable clasps so that only the priest could open them, and that these books were covered in a strange, thin, pale leather, which many then said would have been made from the skin of unbaptised infants, and that these books would be grimoires: books of magical instruction wherein were set down the secrets of demonic evocation, necromancy – the raising of the spirits of the dead to learn the future – spells of invisibility and shape-shifting and all manner of abominable idolatries and hideous blasphemies. *Unspeakable things.*

From this mire of whispered imaginings there then arose a horror all too real, for a child from a nearby farmstead went missing. Searches were made far along the coast in both directions, as well as of the surrounding countryside. Whenever the searchers looked towards the kirk, there atop the tower, like a black crow, could be seen the priest, watching them. If only their eyesight had been sharp enough they would have discerned the wisp of a smile playing across his thin, closed lips.

No trace of the child was ever discovered.

The following months came and went and when, save for the child's immediate family, the sense of shock and loss was just beginning to ease a little, it happened again. This time a boy from the village itself was missing. Searches were made as before but there was no sign. Now the village began to be gripped by a feeling of dread, tighter and tighter. None spoke what all were thinking and fearing lest talking of it might make it happen. All joy was quite overshadowed by that tension that knew no relief when a third child went missing. Now many said that they were under a curse, a curse that was God's punishment for all the wicked talk and gossip that had gone on in the last few months. Whether every villager believed this or not, they all certainly felt that evil was now in their midst, an evil that went on for three years, a silent horror, where children's lives seemed suddenly ended, for they were just gone. They could not be laid to rest for no bodies were ever discovered. All that was to be found was an aching unknowing, a gaping uncertainty.

The priest had for some time been suspected of being the cause of this grief; he was a stranger in their midst, whose manner and nocturnal visits to the kirk made him seem strange and inhuman. And, priest though he was, it was not difficult to suspect him of evil practices. Were not priests more prone to the spiritual sins of sorcery and black magic? For priests could read and understand what was written in books – and their priest had books. Once exposed to demonic and infernal influences, what depravities might not even a priest descend to?

They decided to watch the kirk, by day and by night. Two villagers would watch from several places where the kirk's doors could be observed. After an hour or so, others would take their place. Then, one midnight, their determination was rewarded: a villager stared for a moment in disbelief; there was the priest carrying a limp body over his shoulder, whose long hair hung over her face like a pall. He shouted to raise the alarm and ran at the priest but the kirk door boomed shut and the bolt scraped to.

Soon the whole village was at the door, those nearest beating at it with axe and mell before stepping back, making way for others hurrying through the crowd with a small tree trunk to batter the door down. The noise outside made the silence from within, save for the dull resounding of the make-shift battering ram, seem all the more eerie. After some time, the door finally began to give way to the sound of splintering wood. At last the bolt was heard to be torn from its place and clang on the stone flags within. Once inside, tapers were lit, but there was no

movement save for those unsteady flames that reflected a dull
flickering from the cold, stone walls. There was no one there.

They heard shouting from outside, for the priest had appeared
behind the tower wall, his face framed by a dark cowl pulled
over his head. He shouted like a man in triumph:

"Now you shall see something!"

He flung wide his arms and began to throw words to the
firmament:

Legions of Hell's infernal layers,
I conjure you by art, not prayers!
Astaroth and Belial,
Make this place a living hell!
Let slip a storm of unearthly power
That makes these sheep before me cower.
Their souls are full six days unshrived;
Cease not the blast 'til they're buried alive!
Pile high the sand so nothing can thrive,
A monument to my proud crime,
And let it stay thus throughout all time:
Of Satan's might, a dreadful sign!

In answer came a great crash of thunder and sheet lightning brought a second's daylight, wherein all saw clearly the
priest vanish – not duck down behind the tower wall but just
suddenly gone like a ghost at cockcrow. Now the wind took
up with a mighty roar that pressed them against the walls of

the kirk. Some managed to gain a door for shelter whilst others were thrown against the walls of their homes of creaking wood; even now the thatched roofs were being torn up and whipped away and horizontal streams of sand blasted their eyes blind and their skin raw; the waves seemed alive as they jostled in a rush to storm the shore and, overhead, crackling lightning whipped and goaded the wind, sea and sand to a greater and greater fury. On and on it went.

Some say it went on for nine days and nights. But when the wind finally fell, dawn could be seen in the east. Forvie strand lay storm-shocked and wind-wrecked.

Strange and new: great hills of sand distorted beyond recognition what should have been familiar to the fishermen sailing north later that day past Forvie Ness. A short while later, beyond Hackley Bay, passing Broadhaven, they saw that the storm had even torn down parts of the cliffs to expose a cavemouth. One thought he could hear cries. They all strained to listen, then heard them too. When they at last reached the place, they thought her at first a mermaid, bound at the wrists and ankles, covered in sea wrack. She could not speak, only shake and cry out. Her eyes led theirs to the final horror, for the girl's gaze was fixed further within the cave. There the mystery of Forvie was laid bare. Twelve small naked skeletons, some still with shreds of flesh, flaps of skin and strands of hair, lay in a heap, piled like rubbish.

Some now lit tapers and explored further within the cave. A passage was found which stretched on for a good mile, as they reckoned, until it opened into a small square chamber against one wall of which stone steps led to a wooden trap door. When they tried to open the door they could not, for the amount of sand above; it was bowed with the very weight of it.

It seems that the priest had discovered this passage and tunnel. When the girl at last recovered her senses, she told that, before leaving her there that fateful night, the priest had relished telling her that if he did not return, she would starve to death in the cold and dark, and that if he did return, she would be offered as a sacrifice to the Evil One and share the same fate as the other Forvie children. Now she alone of Forvie's folk was alive.

What became of that foul priest no one knows. His curse changed Forvie forever. Yet, it has abated with the centuries. Gentler winds have now exposed the ruined walls of Forvie Kirk to view once more, and things alive are again seen on her shore. Each spring, terns and eiders lay their eggs and raise their young, and heather blooms, and bees hum.

THE KEEP

Kirsty Logan

We started with a ring. We thought she would like that. When she opened the drawer and saw the ring there, reclining gleamingly on a hank of pink silk, her face opened up sunny-joyful. We knew that she thought it was from him. That couldn't be helped.

She put it straight onto her finger. We watched her toy cattish with it for the rest of the day, twisting it to and fro as she swooned and hummed around the caravan. When she'd first arrived she'd moved slyfoot, placed teacups down with fretting care, each step tightroping. We knew why. When we'd first arrived, we'd seen the way the little tin caravan sat high in the tree, bound to the thick oak branches, hung flimsy-like over a fast-flowing burn. We'd all moved slyfoot then too, at first. We had not wanted to make the caravan fall clatter-crash out of the tree. But soon we settled, just as she was settled, and her steps fell hard as hail. That was when we crept out of our hiding places.

To and fro, to and fro she twisted the ring. She cleaned in time with her songs, finding pretty nooks for all the things that needed tidied away. A pint of milk, a pink slinking nightgown, a dustpan, a pair of toothbrushes. The caravan was a labyrinth of hidings: drawers and cupboards and little sneaky nooks. Finally she felt the words spark scratchy on her skin. She frowned, pulling off the ring to peer at its innards. Until I die. She rubbed where the etched words had caught her. If we had had breath, we would have held it.

We watched her frown a realisation, then release it in fear of wrinkles. We knew as well as she did that he would not stand for wrinkles. Perhaps the ring was not a gift from him after all. Perhaps she'd stumbled on the remnants of old loves. But whose? Until I die – and he was still alive.

She tried to open the drawer and hide the ring. But that drawer would not open again today. She tugged and she coaxed, but the drawer stuck fast. Finally she hid the ring in her face cream, dropping it in and shaking the little pot until it was submerged. We watched as she opened and opened and opened the bathroom cupboards until she found one the perfect size, its edges kissing the face cream pot as she slid it in. Such tininess in the caravan, but always somewhere to be secret.

When he came home, she greeted him with neat kisses. We hid in the smallest cupboard and listened. There was no talk of gifts. Her finger was swollen where the words had scratched, but he did not notice. Outside the caravan the rain shushed and the wind throbbed and the moon blinked bright. Inside, time stopped. The chattering burn stole all sound; the spreading leaves took all sight.

After dinner he used his petty magic to transform the couch into their bed. They lay together. We wished that we still had hands, so that we could cover our ears.

The next day, after he had left, we tried again. A hair ribbon. Plush velvet, thick as wolf fur, red as a heart. She found it while trying drawers in search of washing-up gloves. She forgot about the dishes and reached for the ribbon. It curled lovingly into her hand, and with a turn she bumped the drawer shut with her hip. She pulled back her conker-shining curls with one hand, the other ribbon-busy.

But... a tickle on her fingersides. She stopped and peered. Three hairs twist-tangled in the ribbon, ever so long and ever so blonde. We watched her look at the hairs. We watched her stroke the blood-red ribbon. We watched her fingers come away wet. With a cry she dropped the ribbon and kicked it away from her.

She didn't try to open the drawer again this time. She knotted and knotted and knotted the ribbon and she opened her underwear drawer and pushed it right to the corner, covering it up with her fripperies and frills.

When he came home they ate in silence. Her fingertips were stained red. They went to bed, and we had no need of covering our ears. In the darkness we heard the click-clack of her thoughts.

We watched her open the drawer four more times in four more days. We left her a silken negligee delicate as mothwings, a pair of stockings twisted garrotte-thin, eyelashes faded grey and crumbling, painted fingernails with fleshly scraps caught at their bases. And on the seventh day, we left her a heart.

We watched her open the drawer as though she were looking into a lion's mouth. She'd turned slyfoot again. Despite the labyrinthing, she was running out of places to hide our things. She pulled back when she saw the heart, enthroned in the drawer among a scatter of dried roses. It shivered in a single beat. She leaned in. Perhaps she thought it was a kitten, buttersoft and full of mewls. Perhaps all these gifts were from him after all.

We watched her lift out the heart. She held it in her hands. She squeezed it. Hard. The flesh bulged around her fingers. Of course she did not think it was a kitten. Now we understood her thoughts and her insides as if her skin were made of glass.

He'd taken a caravan, a portable shelter, ordinary as dirt – he'd taken it and magicked it into a labyrinth for girls, a make-believe home the size of eight coffins lashed together. Some girls escaped, but we didn't. We ignored the signs, or the signs weren't there. We'd got lost and we'd never been found. Our tangles of hair, our bright scraps of frock: tossed up into the trees, to be worked into birds' nests. Our straight white bones and our tender mauve organs: dropped down into the burn, carried out to sea. He thought that was the end of us.

She spoke to us then. She told how he had found her. Rescued her. Claimed her. Made her see that the world was cold and dark and hard and empty – but with him, life would be delicious, abundant. He'd put his hands over her eyes, and when he took them away she saw differently. The happenings before him were too hard to focus on, furled and dark like sun-damaged film. All she could see was his face.

We know, we cried, though she could not hear. We all knew his face. It was the last thing we'd seen. We shouted that it would be the last thing she'd see too. He'd tear out her heart just so he could hold it in his hands. He'd throw the remnants of her to the trees and the sea.

Some of them ran long before reaching the heart. Some of them ignored its urgent throb, staying until they couldn't leave. But for her, this was enough. She dropped the heart. With her bloodied hands she tore open the door. She ran away.

We knew she wouldn't be back. We slipped back into the littlest cupboards and waited for him to come back to his crowded, empty home.

THE GHOST WIFE

Gauri Raje

This is a story from South Asia, where relationships between a mother-in-law and a young wife can be particularly strained at the beginning. Moreover, there are different kinds of ghosts and spirits that inhabit particular kinds of trees and strike bargains or kidnap bodies of unsuspecting folk to live among the human world.

There was once a wife of a learned man who had a strange encounter.

There was once a ghost who got to live a human life, just for a while.

The wife of the learned scholar was a simple woman, living with her husband and mother-in-law, just as many other wives did in her village. But her husband loved his books, and knew each of the pages more than he knew her. Her mother-in-law seemed to recognise her only as a pair of extra hands in the house. And the dutiful daughter-in-law worked hard and long, her skin growing pale and her body thinner with each passing day.

One day, she was at the village well, as usual – cleaning the clothes, washing the utensils and filling pots of water. Exhausted on her way back, she leaned against a tamarind tree for a breath. There was a small curve in the bark of the tree where she rested her head. In that moment, a white mist of a hand seemed to reach out and hold her by the neck.

"Aieee!" she began to scream, but no voice seemed to emerge.

"Hello there!" a voice from behind her began. "I have been watching you for days. Ah, don't look back. Just listen to me," said the voice, pleasantly conversational.

The voice put forward a proposition. Would she trade a few days with the ghost of the tree – a sankchinni? The sankchinni was tired of being cooped up in the tree quite alone. No one even came near the tree, believing it to be occupied by a ghost. Since the wife had turned up, the sankchinni had taken the opportunity to leave the tree. The life of the woman seemed quite pleasant indeed. She dressed well, she was slim and pretty and she had a husband. The sankchinni thought she had it all.

The dutiful wife did not think this was a bad bargain at all. A few days of rest and peace would allow her to gather her thoughts. And a bargain was struck. The ghost took the wife's body and the wife's soul rested in the tree among the gentle winds by the well.

When the ghostly wife returned to the house, no one seemed to notice any difference. The husband found his wife more lively than before, and the mother-in-law thought the wife had a spring in her step now and was glad for it. But, in a few days, the changes in her daughter-in-law were quite apparent. Instead of the weak and exhausted wife, the mother-in-law found the wife to be remarkably busy. All the housework seemed to be completed in a very short time. The husband seemed contented – instead of a wife who bothered him for attention, she had suddenly become engrossed with housework, singing and generally keeping out of his way. Neighbours were a bit surprised to discover the young wife bringing food to their house, chatting them up and having time to help their wives with their chores. The young wife was becoming quite popular in the village.

The sankchinni was having the time of her life. She quite forgot about the trade of a few days with the actual young wife.

The soul of the young wife, quite rested now, was getting a bit lonely and bored. Every time the ghostly wife came to the well, she tried to call out to her. However, there could be no communication until the ghostly wife rested near the tamarind tree, and the ghostly wife seemed to be doing her best to avoid the tree.

As days went by, the mother-in-law began to notice that the wife seemed to be taking much less time to fetch things from each room in the house than she used to. She asked her son, but he was quite content with the way things were. One day, the mother-in-law was sitting in her room and suddenly sensed a hand opening the drawer of her dresser. She looked at it out of the corner of her eye, not wishing to make a sound. A hand with the bangles of her daughter-in-law had come through the wall of the room and was holding a bottle of hair oil, and then withdrew to the next room. As the mother-in-law went past the next room, she saw her daughter-in-law sitting in her room, oiling her hair, with a bottle of hair oil in her hand.

The mother-in-law was quite suspicious, and very spooked. She spoke to her son, who seemed quite content with the liveliness of his wife. To confirm her suspicions, the mother-in-law sought the advice of an ojha – a person who can recognise ghosts and spirits in human form. The ojha asked her if her daughter-in-law had an aversion to turmeric, for that is what ghosts cannot bear. So, the next morning, the mother-in-law mixed a little bit of turmeric with herbs and fresh cream – a mixture that they would use to keep their skin smooth in the cold weather. She put some on her own face and left a bit for her daughter-in-law. When the sankchinni put the cream on her face, she screamed as it bit into her skin.

With her skin burning, the sankchinni ran to the well to soothe the burning with well water. The water soothed the burning somewhat, and, tired, the ghost in the wife's body sat at the foot of the tamarind tree to rest. In that moment, the soul of the actual wife caught hold of the ghost in her body and reminded her of the trade of a few days.

Even for ghosts, a word given is a bond. The ghost, moreover, had no desire to return to a house where turmeric was applied to one's body. Gratefully, they changed back to their roles, the wife in her human body and the ghost back into the hollow of the tree.

On returning, the wife looked at her anxious mother-in-law.

"Shall I make the potatoes as you like them — with a top sprinkling of turmeric?" she asked.

Later that day, over a long and contented lunch of dry potatoes with turmeric, chapatis and dal, the daughter-in-law related her bargain with the ghost to her mother-in-law. And from that day, the mother-in-law made sure that the daughter-in-law was treated as a person in the house, not just a pair of hands to do the housework.

I LIVE ALONE

Conner McAleese

The TV always plays what I want it to. I can walk around in nothing but a smile and talk to myself, about myself, at myself in the mirror. I can put on voices and shout "DOVAGERIS!" like I am Daenerys Targaryen. I can cry on the hall floor when I come home from work. I can make southern fried chicken at half three in the morning. No one can judge me. No one knows. I can watch the couple across the street without anyone's interference. Without anyone calling me weird. I'm not weird. I'm not. I just like to watch. To remind myself that there's a world outside midnight feasts and crying. A world with rules. I like rules, but I don't have any.

I see her wake up in the morning. I sit by my window, three stories up, and pretend to read a book while she opens her blinds. I usually like to walk around the house in a blanket. Sometimes it is draped around me like I am Anne Boleyn, freshly coronated Queen of all England. Other times I wear it like a cloak around my head and I am Anakin Skywalker marching into the Jedi Temple. But I don't wear it while I'm at the window. She might notice me then. And if she saw me she'd know I was watching. And people that know they're being watched don't act like they're invisible. They don't wear blankets over their heads.

She disappears into the kitchen or bathroom or whatever rooms face the opposite street. I see the light flicker on as a bulb nears the end of its life. I can see her shadow move across the floor, the gentle absence of light an indication where she is and what she's doing. I imagine her filling a kettle with water from the tap. She places it in its nest and flicks on its tail. I bet she has a coloured one. I have a coloured one. Purple. Hers would be red. Or maybe amber. In my mind, she reaches into the fridge as the water begins to bubble. A lemon, yellow as a daffodil and shaped like an egg. Slice, slice, slice. She...

She's back.

She's clutching a family bag of crisps in her arms and a large bottle of coke. Piggy bitch. Could she not just have green tea? Maybe her boyfriend wouldn't tote around that thin, blonde girl if she switched to tea.

That was mean. No. I shouldn't have said that.

"I am kind. I am grateful. I am nice."

"I am kind. I am grateful. I am nice."

Once more?

"I am kind. I am grateful. I am nice."

I pretend to read my book. But I peek at her over and over. Eventually she stands up and closes the blinds. But she hasn't noticed me. She couldn't have. She's just going to watch a film. Yeah, that's it. A film. A film in the dark.

I stand up to make tea and see it again. Moving just outside where I can see. A little dark rabbit that laughs at me while I sleep.

"Run rabbit, run rabbit, run, run, run," I sing as I go towards the kitchen.

There!

It moved, slipping into the bedroom.

"Run rabbit, run rabbit, run, run, run."

I open the biscuit cupboard where I keep the rattling tub and feel something watching me.

"BANG!"

I turn and stick my fingers out like guns.

"Bang goes the farmer with his gun, gun, gun. He'll get by, without his rabbit pie."

The bottle lid falls off and I shake the hard little pellet into the palm of my hand.

"So run rabbit, run rabbit, run, run, run."

The bin stinks. I can smell it from here. I let last week's chicken go bad and haven't taken it down to the black bins outside yet. I have to. I can't bear it anymore. I march to it, soldiers on either flank, no rabbit following me this time, and pull the bin liner up and out. I ignore the clang of half a dozen wine bottles – I'm not supposed to drink, you see – and tie it up tight. I'm in pyjamas, bright blue and obvious, but I don't care. I grab my keys and shove my bare feet into dirty trainers and head downstairs. Wait. No. Leave the blanket. And I'm off again.

Outside is weird and horrible. It's wet, which I like, but there are people walking up and down the street, junkies with Chihuahuas chasing them as they stumble along the pavement and students wearing shorts and grinning big stupid fucking grins. Idiots.

"Hey," I hear someone call. "Hey you. Pervert."

I hear the boyfriend hush the girl, telling her he'll sort me out. I laugh. Honey, if you could sort me out then you deserve a…

"I'm talking to you. Come here."

I laugh again. And so I walk across the street, quite unbothered by the ranty little man, ready to ask him all about the blonde girl. That'll show him. Though do I want to hurt Piggy like that? Happy people don't have crisps and coke for breakfast.

His face is red and scrunched with self-righteousness. His hair is wet with rain and damp on his forehead. She's hiding behind him in the close. Her eyes afraid. Much more afraid than she should be. Maybe she has a rabbit too?

"Hey, you and your friend better stop looking in on us."

That catches me short.

"My friend?"

"Yeah. You and your fucking friend better stop watching us. Pair of creeps."

"What do you mean 'friend'?" I hear myself say but the familiar dread darts like a hare up my spine.

Run rabbit, run rabbit, run, run, run.

114

"Him," the girl says as her boyfriend looks at me like I'm crazy. He's not so tough now. She's pointing upwards. I follow her finger and turn towards my flat. My little slice of somewhere safe in such an unsafe world. And I see it. The fingers disappearing behind the curtains as they pull themselves out of sight.

POSSESSED BY RAVENS

Daru McAleece

The towers were burning, heat searing his face. He ran from the tower block, bare feet slapping onto cold concrete, escaping the conflagration. He gazed through a wire mesh window and in the night all was aflame. He tried warning others, but there was no answer and desperation filled him. Turning, he suddenly awoke – he was opposite the lifts, and their warped metal doors scratched their way open. His mind reeled as under the dim light an incomprehensible blue-black apparition appeared: a giant crow-headed figure dressed in tattered robes soaked in a film of dried blood. He felt numbed as it slowly walked towards him, spreading arms and wings in a great gesture. Its eyes fixed him, rooting him to the spot. Terrified, his mind felt afire. It bowed oddly, then, cawing and popping, it screeched:

"Praise the multitude!
There will be a slaughter!"

Immediately it vanished and his mind was filled with pictures of forbidding grey landscapes. All was waste and dust. Despair was in his stomach and his head was hollow. Reaching down he tried grasping the dust, but it was so fine it ran from his hands. He blinked and the scene suddenly flickered away – he was standing in his floor's empty drying area in the pale dawn with damp clothes hanging around him like cold ghosts. The strange creature's voice echoed on the wind:

> *"The Awen foretells, the day will come,*
> *Let this be the speech of Afagddu..."*

Trying to shake the nightmarish visions from his head and feeling cold, he slowly walked back to his mother's flat. His right hand was clenched hard. He uncurled it and there, like a powerful totem, was the door key, along with its deep red impression in his palm. The front door was wide open and he realised he'd left it unlocked again. As he crept into bed, red LEDs blinked 3am at him. Exhausted, he fell back to sleep.

"Owen! Owen... it's late!"

Slowly, his mother's voice called him from the depths he was lost in. What day was it? This was happening more now – strange figures appearing, weird chants, darkness on the land and a sense of ruin and death in the world. He was not feeling content with his life, was tired of the apparitions, and had no clue what was happening. But as they disturbed him, something in these strange figures also called to him.

"Owen! Breakfast!"

"There will be a slaughter..."

Resentfully he chucked on stale clothing and wandered to the kitchen. His mother was there, gazing out the window. The sun was gently rising and he saw tinges of delicate golden light touching the fields. The view was beautiful, peaceful.

"Dunno why you make me breakfast. Can get my own," he muttered.

She exhaled. "Look. It's been years since you gave up uni. Done. Fine. And there's jobs going at the biscuit factory today."

Eating as fast as he could, he shrugged. She carried on.

"Owen. I thought you'd be doing more by now. You're wasting yourself and I don't like it. I need you to contribute."

He knew she was right, and pretended to care, nodding but carrying on eating.

"Right. You're going this morning, you're doing it," she said firmly. "Get that down you and get yourself going," she said, now smiling and tilting her head how she always did.

"Bye," he said, nodding, giving a quick hug. He put on fresh clothes and dashed out.

Longing for air, he thought he'd go walk, let his mind and body wander directionless. He decided against the interviews – there was no point. Avoiding the lift, he found the stairwell lights were still broken and began stumbling down the steps. Out the corner of his eye, he noticed the walls were covered with scrawls. Looking again, he saw a repeated pattern:

Praisethemultitude!Praisethemultitude!Praisethemultitude!Praisethemultitude!

Panicked, he jumped down the final steps and threw open the main doors, gasping for air as spots of light danced before him. The all-pervading sickly-sweet smell of biscuits filled the air and he felt desperate to escape. He walked past empty playgrounds and his old primary school, oddly clad in corrugated metal. During hot summers its walls scalded children, and he recalled receiving his head injury as another child pushed a blackboard onto him, putting him into a coma for days. He veered past rusted white barriers, down underpasses tunnelling below perpetually busy carriageways. Wandering, he found himself among partly demolished stone tower blocks. Looming suddenly was a grey, empty health centre, in front of which a huge stone statue of a mother-goddess stood holding a child. He reached out, stroking its weathered, rain-marked surface. His skin crawled as he heard stone scraping on stone and the statue's eyes opened. "No!" he thought, trying to turn, but its stone arm gripped him and stone on stone groaned:

"I am the mother of the stars... Afagddu denied my gift, fell into utter darkness..."

She was white like the moon and from one hand blew white dust in his face. Again, flashes of blighted landscapes. She screeched:

"The cauldron is cracked! The land is poisoned! The cauldron is cracked now and forever!"

She dropped his hand and he wiped dust from his face.

Looking up, pockmarked stone arms cradled a child. All was as it had been.

He strode away, adrenaline eventually subsiding, and found the green fields he loved. Here paths and streams flourished that were buried by concrete elsewhere. More importantly, apparitions and roads felt far away. He gazed up at the sky and breathed out as a lark sang – in the far distance was a Bronze Age burial mound. As his mind found space he tried grasping what was happening to him, but felt lost. He pulled up stones and exposed soil, but insects only scurried away from him. He felt a longing for leaving everything, just running, that he'd never felt before. Was he cursed? He didn't know.

In the late evening sun he saw translucent silken carpets across the fields. Looking closer, he saw that they were spider webs, and that even barbed wire fences had been delicately wrapped and softened. Grasses swayed in undulating patterns in the breeze, helping his mind find calm, and he lay down to sleep deeply for the first time in months. When he awoke, he felt cold and damp, unsure if he'd slept all night or not. Walking towpaths, he slowly followed the canal filled with rushes, rusting metal and wildlife back towards the estate.

Days later, Owen lay in bed for what felt like hours, trying to empty his mind. His mother's call brought him back. Sitting with her, she seemed like a blur, there in front of him asking about the interview.

"Any news yet?"

"Wasn't successful," he lied.

He watched as his mother's face seemed to flutter and dissolve, and the revealing scene before him swam into an odd clarity. In his vision, he was on a windy hilltop. Figures approached dressed in old military garb. One shouted:

"Iolo Morganwg! Cease this gathering or we will open fire upon you! By order of the King these gatherings are a crime!"

Beside him there were others dressed in linen robes marked with symbols of three lines, like rays of the sun held in a circle. Together they recited a prayer:

"God, impart Thy strength."

The soldiers confronted them.

He could still hear his mother saying: "Owen, please. Why are you ignoring me? I don't know what's gotten into you – did you really go?"

"And in strength, power to suffer," the chanting continued, as the soldiers approached.

"Are you listening?" she shouted.

"And to suffer for the truth." The soldiers raised their weapons.

"Owen. I'm worried about you. Sometimes you disappear."

"And in the truth, all light." "Take aim!" they shouted.

"I think you need help. Medical help. Your attacks have started again," she whispered.

"And in light, gwynfyd." The soldiers hesitated.

"Please, Owen!" she pleaded.

He could not see her, but he heard her.

"And in gwynfyd, love." The soldiers lowered their weapons.

"I'm worried. I want to help."

"And in love, God." The soldiers got back onto their horses.

"And I love you," she said, holding his hand.

"And in God, all goodness." The soldiers turned and rode away, leaving the party unharmed.

The vision faded.

Owen rose up, afraid and shouting: "Mum! I've no idea what's happening! I don't want this anymore! I don't want this life!"

She jumped up to go to him, but he ran out the flat, slamming the door, leaving his mother there stunned and worried.

The dusk crows cried and he sprinted for the trees. He ran to the knoll, the patch of trees between the towers and the canal where he'd played as a child. There he could hide. His mother would be phoning 999 believing he'd relapsed. He walked past elder and blackthorn where tattered carrier bags hung limp like bleached prayer flags. It seemed to be taking him longer than normal to find his hollow. Slowly it dawned on him that he was on paths he had never seen before. Paths where there should be no paths. He realised he was now lost in a vast dark wood that should not exist. Grass became lush and wood became wild. He heard wailing and was unsure if it was sirens or animals. The wood pressed upon him, huge, knowing and ancient. This woodland should not exist – it was not here. It was dead. It was not here – it terrified him. At its mercy, he kept walking into darkness. Through the wild, ancient oaks, cathedrals of beech and chestnut, he saw a glimmer of light. There was a fire. As he approached, he saw a great clearing. Motionless and apart from the fire stood a tall, robed figure. Fearfully he approached.

The apparition sharply raised its head, looking right at him, bidding him to sit by the fire. In silence they sat for some time. He gazed at the circle of trees standing like a silent parliament. The apparition broke the quiet, intoning a strange and wordless chant that felt like it called to both the deeps of the earth and the lonely stars. It arose out of primordial time and sang the non-human songs of the minerals and plants, and it chilled the depths of his soul.

"Owen. I have many names and many forms."

Intermingled and jarring, the shade changed before his eyes.

> *"I am One of Three Slaughter Blocks of Ancient Britain.*
> *I am Afagddu – Utter Darkness.*
> *I am the Great Sea Crow!"*

The crow-headed spirit from the lift appeared. He moved to run, but it vanished.

"What are you?" he screamed.

Full of fire and darkness, the Druid instantly was by him shouting:

"Owen! I am the last of the Druids! My spirit in battle was torn from my body and assigned to this, the ancient forest of Caledon. The wildwood."

The apparition was at his face.

"The Romans destroyed us, slaughtered on Anglesey – see!"

Immediately the grove swam before his eyes, transforming into a place of death. Pieces of corpses were scattered about the trees and grass, torn apart like bird food. White robes and grass were both red. Owen begged for the carnage to vanish. The Druid shade gestured and spoke.

"In another time I was to receive a gift from my mother's cauldron – it was stolen. I sat there despairing, gazing at twisted shards of the broken cauldron. Amongst poisoned land and dead horses I gazed deep into darkness and I gained another gift, not inspiration but the gift of Baleful Knowledge. Knowledge of the future – your future."

"What do you mean, my future?" said Owen.

The Druid's shadow breathed by him.

"The grave of the saint is vanishing from the altar-tomb – your future is inescapable. You bring yourselves to the ending of things – devastation urges onward."

The Druid tapped his forehead. Before his eyes, Owen saw and felt the full meaning of the scorched desolate wildernesses he had seen. This was indeed the future of all life on earth – all would turn to dust and death.

"Is there a way out of this world, this future?" Owen asked. "I have never felt a part of it – never wanted to live this life."

"Yes, if you desire it. There is a way to step out of the circle to what is hidden, returning to what once was," the Druid whispered. *"Do you truly desire this? This is a hard covenant."*

Owen nodded. "Yes."

"Then, I salute thee, bard of the border – there is no returning from this path, but may you find peace from the storm within, finally."

The Druid raised his hands and chanted a mysterious sound that echoed through the night. Out of the dark trees came a great white stag, its tines twisted like oak branches. The stag walked up to Owen, directing him to follow. Glancing at the Druid, who nodded, he laid his hand on the stag's flank, walking with it back into the trees. Owen vanished from the circle and the Druid slowly bowed his head, speaking softly:

"The heavy blue chains held the faithful youth,
And before the spoils of Annwvn woefully he sings,
And till doom shall continue a bard of prayer."

After a long search, Owen was finally discovered. He was found dead, sitting upright under a stand of young oak trees behind the towers, though many could not recall such trees being planted. They seemed to have broken through concrete slabs. What shocked everyone more was not only that his body showed no discernible cause of death, but that he was covered from head to toe in an unseasonal layer of white frost.

WHEN WE CREATE OUR OWN GHOSTS

Alycia Pirmohamed

I found her at the narrowest point of the canyon.

I found her at the rift I had dreamt into existence.

In the beginning, she named the swiveling gorge:

a river's hunger, and after a while she called me River.

I carve away the world – it's true.

As soon as night ravels, I open my jaws to eat midnight.

I am a tapestry of darkness that hungers for darkness.

I found her knocking down the world,

but the world soon burgeoned again like a good, long, story.

When We Create Our Own Ghosts

This is an old moral and a new myth.

This is an old grief that plots retribution in a new rain.

Once upon a time, I found her riven with faces.

She wore all the faces that had come before me,

hair astray, millions of eyes: blinking: thick: dark: lashes.

Once upon a time, she dug a grave for every sweet bird

and every sweet birdsong. It was unbearable.

Horrendously, the earth recovered.

I only did this because I am faceless and hungry.

I am the darkness of my own mouth.

Unbearably, I created her. I named her destruction

and she wore the epilogue like a cotton dress.

THE WEE SINGING BIRD

Betsy Whyte

I've never heard anyone telling this they way I tell it, but it's just the same thing, practically.

It's about an old woodman who found a bairn in a craw's nest. A wee laddie. And he took it home to his wife. They already had a wee lassie, you see. And he took it home to her.

She says, "Well," – she didny really want it, you see – she says, "you're an awfy man," she says, "I've plenty with the one I've got."

But anyhow, she brought up this wee laddie. But she was never good to him. She couldny stand him. And the man adored him because he had always wanted a son.

One day, when the man was awa, the wee laddie come in. And he says, "Ma, can I get an orange?"

And she was really fed up of him. She says, "Aye, I'll tell you where you'll get an orange."

There was a great big kist. A great big heavy kist that they used to keep long ago.

She says, "If you go in there, you'll get an orange."

So, he opened this up – it took him all his time to lift this big lid up – and he's bending over to try and get an orange when she *plunked* the kist down on his neck and took the head right off him.

"Oh, there, now," she says.

She took him and she set the head back on again. And she set him out on the porch, and she put a scarf round, you see? And he's sitting there. And the wee lassie come in. Playing about. She was playing with a ball. And she thought it was her brother sitting, you see, and she threw the ball at him. The ball hit him on the head. And the head fell off. Down on the floor of this porch.

She started to scream, and howl, and come running in: "Oh, Maw, Maw, Maw!" she says, "I've knocked my brother's head off! I've knocked his head off!"

"Oh," she says, "you're a *bad girl* for doing that."

"Oh, my daddy'll kill me, my daddy'll kill me."

She says, "Well, I'll tell you what we'll do." She says, "We'll go and bury him underneath that juniper tree down there."

"Will it be alright?"

She says, "Aye, come on." And the woman says, "No, wait a minute." She says, "I don't have much meat in the house. We'll cook him first. And you can bury the bones."

She cooked this wee boy and they had him for supper. Because the man didny ken any better.

But the wee lassie, she was vexed about it, you see, about

her wee brother. She was too young to understand fully what was going on, really. But she lifted all these bones off the plates and she went down and buried them down under the juniper tree.

Now, when she buried the bones there, there was a thing like a wee white dove rose up out of the mist and flew away up in the sky. And it flew about from place to place, sitting on branches here and there, and it would sing:

My mammy kilt me,
My daddy ate me,
    My wee sister Jean,
    She pickit my bones,
And buried them aneath the juniper tree.

It was flying about, flying about saying this all over the place. There were lots of folks saying, "Come back, wee bird, and tell me that again!" So it did it. Lots of different places.

Now, one man says to it, "Have you been all over the place, wee bird?"

It says, "Aye."

The man said, "Come back again!" He was throwing it crumbs and everything that it would like. "I'll tell you what I'll do with you. I'll give you a beautiful string of amber beads if you sing that wee song to me again."

So, the wee bird sat and sang:

My mammy kilt me,
My daddy ate me,
   My wee sister Jean,
   She pickit my bones,
And buried them aneath the juniper tree.

He says, "Sing it again! Go on, sing it again and I'll give you a beautiful watch."

So, the wee bird sang it again.

He gave it the watch.

This man was never tired of listening to this, you see. He'd never heard a bird sing like that before.

"Sing it to me again and I'll give you... what do you want?" he says.

"A millstone."

He says, "What do you want a millstone for?"

It says, "I just want a millstone."

He says, "Alright, I'll give you a millstone."

So, the wee bird sang it again.

My mammy kilt me,
My daddy ate me,
   My wee sister Jean,
   She pickit my bones,
And buried them aneath the juniper tree.

So, the wee bird got the millstone round its neck, and this watch, and this string of amber beads, and it flew on and it flew on, until it come to where his mother and father – well, it was all the father he had – and his sister lived.

And when it got there it started singing on top of the roof, you see, and singing and singing away. And the wee lassie run out.

She says, "Listen to that wee bird, Daddy! Listen!"

The wee bird kept singing the same thing over and over. This woman was sitting and she was cringing, because she understood what the bird was saying, you see. She kent it must be something telling what she'd done. So, she wouldny gang out. And the wee lassie, when she ran out, the bird dropped her the amber beads.

She picked them up.

She said, "Oh, look, Daddy, what the wee bird gave me!"

And it still persisted in sitting there and singing.

And the man says, "I must go out too."

And he went out.

The wee bird flew round about and dropped the watch to him. And still it kept singing.

And the man says, "You go out."

"No, I dinny want to go out," she says.

"Go on," he says, "it might have something nice for you too."

So, in the end, they persuaded her to go out, and the bird dropped this millstone on the top of her and crushed her to pieces.

When she was crushed to pieces, this wee bird transformed into the wee boy again. He was back, alive again.

And that's the end of that one!

POOR ANNA

Max Scratchmann

Shona remembered her first train journey north, barely nine years old, the summer that she had been packed off to Scotland to spend the school holidays with Gran and Great Granny Edith. Little scrap of a child that she was, cowering alone in the compartment that they'd booked for her like a bedraggled evacuee, counting off the stations that she recognised from the faded picture postcards in Mum's old album. Carlisle, Hawick, Edinburgh Waverley. Then over the spidery rust-red limbs of the Forth Bridge and on up to Perth, ticking off Dunkeld, Ballinluig, Pitlochry and Blair Atholl before finally alighting at Garrioch Junction and Gran's loving arms. Seeing the old lady smiling at her from the platform. Her broad-shouldered frame silhouetted in sharp relief against the quicksilver sky of a rainy July day, the familiar scent of Pan Drops still clinging to her heavy sweater as they hugged in the chill wind.

"I still can't believe that I've actually got you to myself for a whole summer," she'd enthused as they bundled Shona's little suitcase into the back of her old blue Austin. "Your mother's very greedy with you, you know, never lets you come up to see me."

"Well, it *is* an awfully long way," Shona had replied in what she felt was a suitably adult tone.

"Aye, well that's what your mother would say, right enough," Gran said mysteriously, slamming the car door, her mouth a tight line.

There was no bridge in those days, and they'd had to sit around in the rain for more than an hour for the chain ferry, Gran buying them both Caramel Logs and American Creme Soda from the post office while they waited, the surface of the loch shimmering when they eventually crossed the singing waters. Then the long drive up the muddy track and the first sighting of Balgair House brooding against the boiling green sky, the whole place in darkness save for a lamp in the upper window where a solitary figure in black stood silent vigil.

Shona had seen many photographs of Balgair House – her mother as a child playing with a ball on the front green, Gran, her hair still dark, beaming over her, maids with their white lace caps peeping from the scullery windows, Granny Edith, a nervous old lady who smelt of lavender water, fretting in the background – but, in the flesh, its formidable grey stone edifice was unlike any structure she had ever encountered on the leafy suburban streets of home, isolated as it was from all other dwellings and lowering up there on the hill like a sour old man jealously hogging his favourite park bench.

"Where have you been, where have you been?" her great grandmother wailed now, pacing up and down and wringing her hands like Uriah Heep as they entered the hall, a scent like mould and wet cement assailing their nostrils. "The water tank has gone and overflowed again and come through the ceiling in the child's room. I don't know where in the world we're going to put her."

Gran made an agitated noise. "Oh, not again," she muttered under her breath. Then, aloud, "We'll just have to put her in Poor Anna's room for tonight, Mother. Shona, you'll be a good girl for me and do exactly as you're told and we'll have everything right as rain in a day or two. You'll do that for me, now, won't you?"

And that was how Shona first learned about Poor Anna.

The room was cold, too cold even for a wet Scottish July, and had a dusty, musty smell to it, much worse than the rest of the house, and, even with the lamp on, it was dark and gloomy with deep pools of shade in every corner. An old doll stared wistfully from the depths of an ancient baby carriage, its pale face a waxy white moon with a dead thing's glassy green eyes; a bedraggled bear peered from another vale of shadow, and, by the deep mahogany dresser, with its perished pier glass, was a dolls' house, the minute slate tiles on its sharply Gothic roof like rows of tiny pincers.

"Whose room is this, Gran?" Shona begged, clutching the hot water bottle she'd been given tightly to her chest with one little hand, the other clinging to her Grandma for dear life. "Why have you put me in here?"

Gran sat down on the bed and kissed her forehead. "You know how this house has been in our family for generations? Well, this used to be your Great Aunt Anna's room. Granny Edith's little sister…"

"But why are all her things still here? All her toys. What happened to her, Gran?"

Gran sighed and smiled a small, wan smile.

"Oh, you would have probably found out soon enough anyway, the way people talk around here. Poor Anna, no one really knows what became of her that night of the awful storm. All we know is that she got up in the wee small hours and wandered out into the pouring rain. They found her the next morning…" She paused, tightening her grip on Shona's hand. "Drowned in the corrie, the poor wee soul. It was a terrible tragedy."

"And Granny Edith's kept her room like this all these years?"

Gran nodded. "Yes. And you must promise me that you'll not touch anything, especially not the toys, while you're here. It's only for a night or two, until I can get Gerard Flett out to repair the water damage next door. You'll do that for me, won't you, Lambie?"

Shona nodded, feeling very small in the big iron-framed bed with its slightly damp mildew-smelling sheets, and Gran kissed her again.

"Good girl. Now, sleep tight and I'll wake you in the morning with hot tea and fresh honey toast."

And then she was gone, turning the light out behind her as she went, the unremitting rain still pounding on the glass outside.

Shona lay alone in the dark. Listening, listening. Tonight, though, all seemed to be silent in this big strange house, the only sounds the gentle stroking of rain on the rattly window panes and the soft chime of the tall clock in the downstairs lobby, sighing away each quarter hour. Then, just when she thought there would be nothing from the two women below, Granny Edith's voice, thin as a whisper, floated like a tiny moth from the warmth of the front room.

"We should have just put her down here. What if they come for her like they did for Anna? What if they come in the night?"

Gran's voice now, sounding impatient: "Mother, that's a fairy story. Nobody came for Poor Anna; she probably just walked in her sleep and went out to the woods. It's tragic, but nothing else…"

Then their voices became muffled again as the old woman paced the room, and Shona could only pick up snippets.

"I kept *you* safe all those years," someone said before a thick and woolly silence. Then Gran again: "Those woods are *not* cursed…"

Then more talk, low and muffled, and she strained her ears, but she was only nine years old and the fear, which had convinced her that she would lie awake all night, was no match for her sheer bone-weariness after today's long journey, and, in spite of everything, she found herself drifting off into a restless sleep, her dreams littered with strange noises and the faint laughter of a little girl she could never see.

It was later, much later, when she woke with a start, the old villa silent save for a soft scraping, scrabbling sound. *Mice*, she told herself, cowering under the heavy blankets. *Old houses like these always have loads of mice, scurrying about behind the walls.* But she knew where the sound was coming from and she knew that it wasn't mice.

Shona, they whispered, shuffling around inside the big old dolls' house, knocking over the immaculate little chairs and tables, their sharp nails rip-ripping at the curtains, tearing nasty cat-claw marks in the perfectly proportioned wallpaper. *Shona, come out and play in the blue, blue moon.*

"Stop it," she whispered from the depths of her hidey-hole. "Stop breaking her things."

Then come out and play with us, they mocked. *Come out and dance in the rain and the blue, blue moon.*

"No," she whispered, pushing her hands over her ears to drown out their song as she burrowed deeper. "No, no, no!"

Oh, come out, they cried, pushing over the teddy bear.

Come out, they laughed, tipping the doll from her rickety perambulator, her brittle china face shattering as she hit the floor. *Come out, come out, come out!*

"Oh, very well," she uttered in fear and exasperation, the music in her soul, the varnished dark-wood floor freezing to her bare feet. "Where do you want me to go?"

Come to the woods with us, they grinned, eyes narrow, mouths full of teeth. *Come to the moonlit woods and meet the Fairy Queen.* And, through the slightly parted drapes, she could already make out the rain-blurred shapes of their lanterns in the trees, honey yellow and sugar pink and tangerine orange, bobbing like fire-flies in the dark, hundreds and hundreds of them, like the tiny glowing creatures in the Walt Disney film she'd gone to see with Gran last summer, their song so sweet that she was desperate to join in the melody.

Come, come, they coaxed.

"I'm coming," she panted, tiptoeing down the stairs and lifting the latch on the heavy wood front door, the soaking gravel of the path cold on her little toes.

Come away, come away, they beseeched, their strings of Hungarian lanterns strewn along the woodland lane.

"I'm scared of the woods," she cried suddenly, tears like tiny ice diamonds running down her pale china cheeks. "I'm scared of it all, I want to go back."

Too late, too late, we cannot return to the Queen's bower empty handed, they hissed like infinitesimal green adders, pinching and nipping at her, their tiny little rodent teeth biting at her legs as bramble branches lashed out and sent her deeper and deeper into the dark, dark woods.

"Let me go back," she sobbed, stumbling on the path, the grass dewy and the fetid scent of the corrie's still water in her nostrils. "Please let me go back."

Too late, too late, their tiny voices whispered on the wind, the shore of the dark tarn strewn with their lights like dew beads on a spider's web. *See, see, the Queen is nigh; she calls you even now to her flowery bower beyond the water's edge.*

And she could hear the song clearly now, hear the words that called her onwards like the sweet arias of mermaids who lured sailors to cold and watery graves upon the rocks. And she knew that she should resist but she could feel herself slipping away like that time in hospital when they had taken her tonsils out and the kindly nurse had shown her how to count backwards. Knew she was slipping as the black waters of the corrie crept up around her legs and made her nightdress billow out around her like a crinoline, the scent of the stagnant water like funeral flowers as it enveloped her. Thick, dark, sweet. Like lavender.

Lavender! She knew that scent of lavender, knew the strong arms around her, plucking her from the water's grasp, her whole body shivering as though interrupted during her first sweet kiss. Granny Edith's voice shouting, commanding them: *Back, back! You shan't have her, not another one, not another one ever!*

And, standing here today in that old house again, so many decades after the bright July morning when the sun had rediscovered Loch Garriochhead and Gran assured her that it had all been a dream – standing here alone with both the old ladies gone, she felt again the unadulterated pull of unfulfilled longing that had plagued her all through a fraught life of failed relationships, unfulfilling careers and perpetual discontent. And the July sun shone and moths fluttered around her head as she flung open the front door. Grasshoppers singing melodies of jubilation and meadow thrush and summer robin alike joining in the creature chorus as she pushed through the thorns and weeds of the overgrown path and found again the still waters of the corrie.

TALA IN THE WOODS

Katalina Watt

When Tala woke, the crimson dawn light was choked by a mist as thick as curdled blood. Her back was curled over, each vertebrate juddering as she unfurled herself with a stretch. She smoothed out her hair and rubbed the warm growing egg of her belly, the creature nestled inside stirring gently. She peered into the mist, hoping it was a sea fret that would soon drive off. There was no way Miguel would risk travelling home in such conditions. She heard the incessant chirping of the crickets and a distant owl's dying hoots. Such sounds usually did not affect her, but this dawn sounded unnatural and her repose was disturbed. She waddled down to the kitchen and tugged at the stiff pantry door, apprehensively eyeing her dwindling supply of tinned goods. Neither of them had expected her ravenousness to surpass the surplus stock they kept in the house, but this was Tala's first pregnancy, and the early nausea had been replaced by an urge for meat. Miguel had hunted as often as he could but as her belly swelled and the seasons changed unfavourably he was shocked to find she had nearly eaten through their provisions.

He had decided on one last emergency supply trip to the village before the rains came and waterlogged the dirt paths, when the horses risked being caught in the mire.

That had been almost a fortnight ago. Tala began to worry that the baby would arrive before Miguel could return, and, despite the books to hand, she shuddered at the idea of birthing her child alone. She hadn't been sleeping well recently; the humidity was unbroken by the rain and mist, and the sheets clung slick to her in the night. Occasionally a cool coastal mist would wash over the house, but every time she moved she felt the weight of her burden pushing at her organs and straining her muscles. Her breasts were sore and swollen and she wept when she dropped a pot. It would be impossible to do this alone, she decided. She needed Miguel, for her sanity.

She tallied the food and calculated she had enough to last out the month. Though the creature wriggled in protestation, Tala forewent substantial meals that day, favouring cool mango and coconut water to drive off the unbearable heat on the back of her neck. That night her body ached for sleep but her mind was crawling up the walls. If Miguel did not return soon, she would be forced to find a way to the village. Even if she was able to birth the child safely and they both survived, they would starve. Tala was a decent hunter when not encumbered with a child, but the rains caused any game to take shelter and she wouldn't risk venturing too far from home.

When her eyelids eventually drooped, sleep came in fitful waves. She stirred, heat prickling between her legs, a pit in her stomach and a heaviness bearing down on her chest. Her throat constricted as everything was silent around her and within her. She rolled her eyes open slowly and looked down at her naked body, the sheet thrown off onto the floor. There was nothing there, save the large swell of the baby.

The next morning, she was alarmed as her hand came away slick with blood in the shower. She cried with relief when her fingers probed and found the source was not her vagina but her navel. A strange confusion came over her, but she was too awash with relief for the child to dwell on it. Perhaps this was a natural part of something pushing against her from the inside.

That night the mist finally lifted, and the striking incandescence of the full moon made Tala ravenous. She pushed her rational thoughts aside, spurred on by the ceaseless kicking of the babe inside, which clawed in hunger, and the noisy cries of her own body. It had been several days since she had feasted properly, and the meagre tinned goods were not enough. She ventured outside the hut where the bright moonlight reflected a pair of eyes. She started and so did the creature, a small mouse deer, which hurtled not away but towards her and became confused, tripping over its own legs and crashing to the ground. Tala held her belly protectively as she surveyed the animal lying still on the grass. She bent to check if the twisted neck had been its demise and raised her hands to her mouth horrified as she began to salivate.

Later, she washed herself, not quite believing that she had eaten it raw with her bare hands. She felt shame hanging over her like a shroud, but she guided that hot flush to a hatred of Miguel. His absence forced her desperation. She didn't understand how he still could not have returned. Now the mist was risen there was no risk of the horses falling on the uneven path, and he would be aware that the rains would soon be upon them. He would not abandon her when the hour was so near. She had to hold to that or she would break. That night, with the mist and humidity relieved somewhat, Tala slept more peacefully. She was full for the first time in many weeks and the baby slept soundly. Sometime in the half-night before dawn, Tala woke to relieve herself. When she returned to the bedroom, she saw Miguel sitting on the bed in the shadows. She screamed, and he rose to hush her.

"It's me, Tala. I'm here."

"What took you so long?"

"I know, I'm sorry. Everything will be okay now."

He held her, and she breathed the sweat and musk of him. He was damp, and his back muscles felt tight and sinewy beneath his shirt, as if they might burst forth from beneath the material.

"Let's go to bed. Everything will be fine in the morning."

He led her to the bed and laid her down gently, kissing her neck and then her swollen belly, and deftly slipping off both their clothes. In the semi-darkness there was something different about him; he seemed leaner, more feline, and his skin tauter than before. He kissed her with vehemence and pinned her to the bed, her belly acting as an anchor, in a way which terrified and thrilled her. It had been so long. He had been away, and before that his concern was all pragmatic and familial. He had not wanted her much and she thought she hadn't wanted it either.

As they lay coiled together in the bedsheets, Tala gripped Miguel's torso and her hands moved across his back. She felt the muscles shifting beneath her fingers and heard the faint fluttering as two huge, dark wings spread open from either side of his back. The moonlight shone translucent through the wings, showing the web-like veins and claw fingers. Tala cried out and shoved the creature away. To her horror the creature split with a violent snap, its upper body above her supported by its arms, and the lower half below the waist still grotesquely pumping away at the air. She saw it as it truly was now, a feminine-shaped bat-like creature. Its face was astonishingly beautiful, with dark hair and bright luring eyes, and it opened its mouth, where a long and proboscis-like tongue slid out towards her navel. The creature was a man-eater and she knew it from folklore of old. In her hunger she had neglected preparations of small pots of rice, which her mother had advised her to use to ward off such beasts, and as Tala looked to it she knew why it had come. She clutched her belly protectively and backed towards the door. The upper half of the manananggal followed her slowly, moving on its strong arms, the beautiful face leering up at Tala from the floor. When she felt the bannister beneath her hand, she turned and fled down the stairs towards the kitchen. She hunted, keeping one eye on the staircase, for the key items she tried to recall from her girlhood superstition. The salt pot was almost empty, and the garlic bulb had only a couple of remaining cloves. She gripped them both with the fervour of the pious, as if these relics could act as holy water or a priest's blessing.

The creature barred the doorway, but Tala ran at it, throwing salt into its eyes. She barrelled into it, forcing it against the wall, and it shrieked as the salt hissed. Tala bounded up the stairs to the creature's lower half, which was still spread on the bed on its knees. She crushed the garlic in her hands and retched as she rubbed the slime along the exposed flesh where the chest had detached. She threw the remaining salt over the creature's lower body and reached to the bedside table where Miguel's ashtray lay. As she grasped it, the torso crashed through the bedroom door, shrieking. Tala threw the ash onto the lower half as the torso jumped upon her, the claws at her face and straining for her eyes. Tala tried to wrench the creature from her and groped around for the discarded ashtray. The manananggal screamed and its snake-like tongue poured forth and descended between Tala's breasts to her navel. As the creature sought entry, Tala's fingers met with the cold stone of the ashtray and she gave a clumsy swing, hitting the creature in the back of the head. It collapsed on top of her; the tongue halted for now.

Tala forced the thing off her and yanked open the curtains, causing a burst of dawn light to penetrate the room. She heard the burning of flesh and the moans of the manananggal writhing in pain, unable to re-join its halves and aflame in the sunlight. Tala could only bear to look long enough to ensure it was truly perishing. She averted her eyes to the growing morning outside, where she spotted a pair of horses and a cart emerging from the nearby forest. She cried with relief to see Miguel in the distance, finally home. A warm wetness poured from between her legs, and Tala panicked as her contractions began, crashing like waves and pulling her under. She called for Miguel, but he was too far away to hear. She felt the creature writhing inside her, and it kicked at the womb lining, pushing the skin out with what almost looked to Tala like a claw instead of a hand.

LAMBKIN

Sheila Kinninmonth

YE'D BETTER WATCH OOT OR LAMBKIN WILL GET YE!

This was often heard by ill-behaved bairns around Kirkcaldy in days gone by. But who was Lambkin?

Well, he was a builder. A very accomplished builder by all accounts – the best in Fife if not Scotland. No one knows his real name but he was called Lambkin because of his mild manners and gentle ways – often more of an insult than a compliment. He was employed by Michael Scott, Laird o' Balwearie, to build an extra tower onto his castle, Castle Balwearie, for his wife, Lady Balwearie, to use as her apartments. She was delighted with her new rooms and immediately moved in. However, when Lambkin appeared at the castle looking for payment, things turned really nasty.

The Laird was reluctant to pay and told the hapless builder, "I dinnae hae the money tae pay ye the noo unless I sell some land and I dinnae want tae dae that and onyway, I maun gang ower the sea for a year but I'll see ye richt when I return."

Lambkin was furious and became a bit unhinged. He had spent years working at the castle, putting up with the snide remarks and nasty nickname. He'd done a good job, the family had moved in and he wanted paid... NOW! All notions of meekness left him as the devil himself seemed to take over, and he uttered a curse on the castle and the family.

My curse be now upon this house,
And on that bairn beside you.
Grim vengeance down shall bear you.
Deserted be the bowers
And empty be the towers
Of the Castle of Balwearie.
The name of Scott shall be forgot
In the Castle of Balwearie.

The wind was howling as the builder left the castle and disappeared into the gloom. Despite the threat and the curse, the Laird just told his Lady to keep Lambkin out of the castle and sailed away on his travels.

But Lambkin had an ally in the house. The nurse who looked after the bairn had a soft spot for him and felt sorry for him. There was no love lost between her and the Lady who employed her, so she chose her moment and let Lambkin in at the side window and lead him into the great hall.

"Whaur are all the menfolk wha cried me Lambkin?" he asked.

"In the far barn at the threshing. It'll be a long time till they come by," answered the nurse.

"And whaur are all the womenfolk wha cried me Lambkin?"

"At the well doing the washing. It'll be a long time till they get back."

"And whaur's the bairns o' this hoose that ca' me Lambkin?"

"They're at the school reading. It'll be the night before they come home."

"And whaur's the Lady o' this hoose, that ca's me Lambkin?"

"She's up in her room sewing, but we soon can bring her down."

A long-held, festering lust for revenge had reached boiling point. He knew what he was going to do. Taking a sharp knife from his belt, he strode over to the bonny baby in the crib and plunged it deep into the small body. The baby began to howl. Lambkin rocked the cradle, making soothing noises, and the nurse began to sing a lullaby, and the blood ran out of every hole in the crib.

The plan worked. They had the Lady's attention.

"What's wrong with the bairn, nurse? Why is he greeting? Still him, put him to the breast," she called.

"I've tried," answered the nurse. "He won't still for that!"

"Try his rattle then!"

"That's no working either," she called back.

"Try the bell then."

"Nothing's going to work until you come down yourself," cried the nurse.

Making her way down the steps, the Lady soon realised what had happened.

"Have mercy on me, Lambkin," she begged. "You've taken my young son's life. Spare mine."

Lambkin turned to the nurse and asked her if he should spare the Lady's life. "Will I kill her or will I no?"

"Kill her," she said. "She's never been good to me!"

And so the deed was done.

Many months passed and the Laird himself returned from his travels to find two dark stains on the floor of the hall.

"Whose blood is this?" he asked, to be told it was the blood of his Lady.

"And whose blood is this?" he asked, to be told it was the blood of his son.

With murder in his heart, he sought out the nurse and the builder. Retribution followed. The nurse and Lambkin were found, and justice was served. Both were condemned to death. The nurse was tied to a stake and burned. Lambkin was forced to suffer a more protracted death, locked in a small room in the tower he built until he starved to death.

NOTE ON THE STORY

Said to date from the fifteenth century, this story was originally collected as a ballad in 1860 by Frances Child. Lord Balwearie lived in his castle near Kirkcaldy, which was gifted to his family in 1463 by King James III.

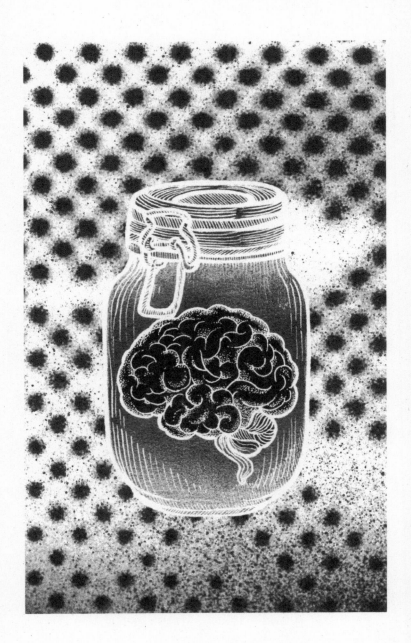

ANNE OF THE DARK EYES

Ricky Monahan Brown

As I record this story, Anne, I am surrounded by this city constructed of towns built upon dead towns and buildings built inside bridges that should not exist. I gaze at the National Monument from atop Nelson's tower. If old Horatio were to peer down through his telescope, he would be quite nonplussed by the facsimile of the Parthenon, that zenith of Doric order, sitting stately and shivering atop Calton Hill. I can imagine the Scottish heroes in the catacombs in the area supporting the main structure of the Monument, and imagine Covenanters birling away under my godforsaken gaze.

I confess that I am recording this story so that I may understand for myself the events set forth herein and the extent of my guilt. No doubt Robbie's maternal grandfather, the old minister, would set me right: I am *entirely* guilty. That I am unable not to sin is proof in itself of the corruption of my nature. From the very beginning of eternity, God has chosen me not to be among those he will bring to himself. But as you weigh my case, Anne, remember that God's choice was not based on the foreseen virtue, merit or faith in the chosen. My damnation does not arise from my vices, nor from my decision to sin. It arises from His choice to deny me His mercy. Robbie's maternal grandfather would be correct, of course. Oh, Anne of the dark curls and the darker eyes, burn this record while you can! If you digest the lessons of my tragic story, you too will see that there is no faith to be had in a God who would choose for anyone the path that has led to my total depravity.

Robbie inhabits the story from the start, of course, just as much as his absence fills its end. It all started, I suppose, in the Dissection Room. We were still nauseous from the night before, he and I, and the steep wooden benches piled vertiginously atop each other threatened to pull me into the forgiving, alabaster arms of the cadaver on the slab below.

"You will note," the Head of Surgery declared with relish, "the burr holes in the skull. One here, an inch and a half above the hairline and an inch to the left of the midline, and another here, an inch to the right of the midline."

"Remind me why we're here again," I groaned to my partner in crime.

It was a rhetorical request. We were law students, not medics. Nevertheless, Robbie had waylaid me outside the Old College, as he so often did. Our late-night roistering had left him too fragile to tolerate the fetid drone of the Dean of the Law School in the stuffy old lecture theatre. So, we had repaired to this cooler, darker room just across the road.

Robbie raised a thin finger to pursed lips and ostentatiously nodded back towards the Head of Surgery.

"This young man complained of splitting headaches at the base of his skull. We quickly ascertained that trepanning would be in order to release the pressure. A simple and routine procedure."

"Routine," Robbie whispered. "You should try that for *your* headaches."

Now I was the one indicating the need for silence.

"…quite surprised when the subject expired during the process. Now, how would you proceed upon such an event? Anyone?"

Robbie louchely unfurled an arm towards the Dissection Room ceiling, as if his long hair and velveteen jacket weren't enough to draw attention to the interloper.

"Yes. You. The Bohemian."

"Well, Sir," Robbie drawled, "I would call for a post-mortem examination."

"Good! Of course you would. And this would be the result."

The Head of Surgery produced a large glass plate with a flourish. Within the plate was suspended what looked like nothing more than a cross-section of a yellowed cauliflower with a hole the size of an apple punched out of it.

"We discovered that the subject had been incubating a brain aneurysm the size of a man's fist. Imagine, if you will, the blood vessel as one of Professor Faraday's rubber balloons, with a bubbling weak spot on the side.

"Going back to the subject's acquaintances, we discovered that not only had he been suffering headaches, but he had also been experiencing vivid hallucinations."

"Do you have that as well?" Robbie enthusiastically enquired.

"No. Don't be ridiculous."

"*Oooooh* – am I even here, or am I just a malevolent hallucination?" he persisted, waving two sets of long, thin fingers across his long, thin face.

"Knock it off," I scolded, pushing him away.

It was a relief when the lecture came to an end. However, my torment had hardly begun as we dashed back across the street with the idea of catching our tutorial. When we turned back into the Old College quad, Robbie – moving at a good clip – practically trampled over the Dean.

"A little late, are you not?" the Dean sneered as he brushed himself down. "Hardly the way one would expect the scion of a respectable family to conduct himself." He looked up at me. "I don't know what you're smirking at. You have potential, boy, but you will be brought low, consorting with wastrels."

Robbie was not one to be sneered at. He might have been ashamed of his well-to-do family, but he was still the heir of a certain haughtiness.

"Sir," he began, fixing the Dean with a cold eye, handing me his cane and delicately removing his gloves. "Sir, I will have you know that maintaining this devil-may-care appearance is not the work of mere minutes. What's more, drinking establishments and brothels across fair Edina will be forced to shut their doors if I am compelled to *waste* my time at your interminable presentations."

With that, he flicked his gloves across the Dean's disbelieving chops.

Time stopped as the Dean spluttered and attempted to regain his authority. I was able to sketch my future history – what a damned curse I was to my parents! I now realised that I had rendered my father's whole life a failure; his hard work and the innumerable second chances he had granted me were all for naught.

Finally, the Dean spoke.

"I do not care who your father or your grandfather might be." His disapproving gaze froze the air between us. "Your studies here are at an end. I will arrange for you to receive a third-class degree in return for you polluting this noble institution no longer. Get out of my sight!"

I pictured my father's ashen face on receiving the news of my failure. What a thing it was to know I had damned the happiness of my parents, probably the only two people who cared a damn about me in the world. In front of us, the agent of that damnation, the Dean, shook with fury, his cheeks the colour of bloodstains on bedsheets from a flea's droppings.

I ceased trifling with Robbie's cane. My impatience was not to be contained. A great flame of anger erupted inside me as if I was possessed. That demon clubbed the Dean to the ground and punctuated my words with the cane's heavy emphasis.

"You – damned – fool! The –Vice – Dean – is – a – good – friend – of – ours – from – the – Speculative – *So – ci – e – ty*. *He* – would – not – be – so – foolish – as – to – bar – me – from – my – studies."

When my ape-like fury finally abated, I became aware of my comrade's horror at the storm of blows and the Dean's audibly shattered bones.

"I don't think the Vice Dean can save you now," he muttered quietly. "I would advise you to go to ground for a while."

With that, Robbie dashed out of the Old College and across the South Bridge and I did as he had advised, for quite some time. Even after the Dean's death had been added to the list of crimes of a scoundrel gambler and housebreaker who had once been thought a respectable tradesman and deacon, I kept away from the gas-lit main streets and scurried along the dark by-streets where the great chocolate-coloured pall of the first fogs of the season would hang low and hide my shame. But in these dark, dismal surroundings I found that I missed my mischievous friend and the intellectual stimulation of my studies. So it was that I found myself, one morning as Edinburgh emerged from a long, brutal winter, buried in clothes that were now enormously too large for me, walking fast, haunted by my fears, back to the scene of the crime. I was almost surprised to find the law school's reception room still where it had sat before the world had been shattered like a dropped mirror.

I bade the receptionist a good morning.

"I wonder if you might be able to help me. I bear correspondence of some importance for a young man whom I believe is a student at this institution. A former classmate of mine, in fact."

I gave the receptionist Robbie's name and she flipped through a card file.

"I'm afraid we have no record of a student by that name, Sir."

"But surely you must. He is hardly a forgettable character. Five feet and ten inches tall; long hair, parted to the right. A glorious moustache and an impish grin. Oh, and prone to... *eccentric* fashion."

I smiled.

"Not unlike yourself, Sir?"

"You are too kind, dear lady! Next to my comrade, I am but a reflection of deformity and decay."

"Well, I am sorry. We have no record of your friend. Now or previously at the college."

I supposed that Robbie's father must have removed him to Europe under the cover of taking some cure for his consumption, and had his record at the University erased. All memories of the unfortunate case were being forgotten, trampled under the feet of our successors. For the first time in some time, I pulled myself to my full height.

"Perhaps you can help me nevertheless. I am a matriculated student here, you see, but have been absent for some time due to ill health. This has left me quite divorced from the latest legal developments, but with a morbid fascination for medicine. I'm wondering if it might be possible for me to effect a change in my studies at this late stage?

"My name? Why yes, of course. It is quite unusual, though."

I spelled my new name for her.

"Henry Jekyll. J-E-K-Y-L-L."

It was as easy as that, and now I am free once again to roam the city and survey it from this telescopic aerie. This city that *claims* to be built on seven hills, like its spiritual precursor. This city built, in fact, on the lies of gentlemen.

I recall now that Playfair and Cockerill's plans for the National Monument never were completed. Edinburgh's Disgrace is but half of what it would otherwise have been, and I love it nevertheless in my own broken way. It is unfinished and stunted, shorn of the imagined catacombs for heroes, but I like to think that it has acquired a power to move as a palimpsest that it could never have had in its completed state. Disabused of its sanctity, the Monument casts aside the repressive effects of the Church and is free *to be!*

It is true, Anne, that I always wanted you to know this story. I can see that now. Now that you know God has chosen total depravity for me, with all that entails for the people amongst whom I live, I know that you – virtuous, forgiving Anne – will be unable to exercise faith in Christ. It is the most virtuous among us, is it not, who must fall the furthest and hardest? I, on the other hand, had not far to fall, and now I can take comfort from the fact that, although I am condemned to suffer everlasting separation from the comfortable presence of God, I am no longer doomed to suffer alone.

THE MAN WITH TWO SHADOWS

Stanley Robertson

Once upon a time there lived a very wealthy man. And this man had a good business, was well respected, and everybody liked him. And his name was Rich John. Everybody liked this Rich John because, oddly enough, when you're wealthy, folk like you. And everybody liked this man. But this man was a kindly man. And he helped his fellow men. He didna like to see anybody in distress, and he never would pass a tramp by without giving him something.

This good fella one day is coming along the road when he notices that he has cast two shadows. So, John says to hisself, "That's funny. I almost feel I've got two shadows." And the two shadows used to merge into one. But sometimes a shadow will do that. He noticed that one shadow was very, very clear, and the shadow that should have been his own was faint. He noticed this for two or three evenings as he was walking home. Until there was one night he just had one shadow. And it was very, very clear and distinct. And he felt his shadow running awa from him. He says, "That's queer."

The next day he went up the road in the evening. He was awa to meet with friends. And he's coming home, and his shadow suddenly just runs awa.

He has no shadow.

He says, "That's queer." He says, "It must be something to do with the light. I canna see no shadow round me."

So, Rich John comes home and he sits in the house, and he's got the strangest feeling, because still he has no shadow. He gings to his bed that night, and when he gings to his bed he hears something fichering about the drawers and fichering about his room. And when he looks up, he sees the shadow, and he says, "This must be a dream I'm having, this canna be real."

In the morning he arose, and he says, "My," he says, "what a realistic dream. I dreamt the shadow was in the room." But when he looks, the drawers have been turned out, his cupboards have been opened…

He says, "Somebody has been in about!"

He noticed that his diary had been read – he used to keep an immaculate diary of things, you know? He noticed it was read. He noticed that pages of his private pages were turned. He looked at the very copy of his will. It was looked at. His blinds – everything private was opened.

He thinks somebody has been in to rob him.

So, that day, as he's going about, he feels there's somebody awfa close by him. The next night, he was walking up the road – he's no shadow at all now – and when he gangs up the stair, his door is open. And when he opens up, there was the shadow, sitting in his armchair.

Rich John gings and says to it, "What are you doing here?"

He says, "It's *all right*, John. I'm a good friend of yours. I've come to stay."

John says, "But I live alone," he says. "I don't have anybody staying with me. I like seclusion."

The shadow says, "Oh, but John," he says, "I've come to you. And I'm going to be a friend of yours."

He starts giving John very interesting conversation. And John was very interested in him.

So, days pass, and this man is in his house. The shadow.

He speaks to the shadow, and the shadow tells him. He plays cards with the shadow. He plays chess with the shadow.

But, every day, this shadow was getting thicker, and more dark, and there was, oddly, a change coming upon the shadow. But John's complexion was getting thinner, and more shallow, and pale, and he wasna so strong as he used to be.

Now, as the days pass by, John was going to his business, and people were speaking to him, and he was doing things. And this day, this man says to him, "Oh, John," he says, "I thought you were away home?"

He says, "Home? Why would I be away home?"

"You said you weren't feeling very well, so you came in early and you done the work you were doing."

John says, "I've never been near work…"

So, he gings home, and here's the shadow sitting doing the books.

He says to the shadow, "Were you at my work today?"

He says, "Oh, yes," he says, "I was at your work. Helping. I want to ken *all* about you." He says, "I would like to know the things that you do."

John says, "Well, don't do things without consulting me. The next time, if you're going to do anything, let me ken. And you can come with me."

So, as the time goes on, this shadow is becoming more like John, until, almost, they're like identical twins.

The shadow starts going out.

Now, John is going to get married. To a very, very wealthy lady. And she lived in another land. John says, "I'm going on holiday to see my sweetheart."

Rich John goes away – gets people to look after his business – but when he gets to this place, this rich lady says to him, "What are you here for?"

He says, "I'm here to see you."

She says, "You were here last week. You said you were going home?"

He says, "But I wasn't here last w—"

She says, "*Don't be stupid.* You're being silly. Of course you were here last week."

He says, "Well… I'm here now. I'll stay here."

She was still pleased to see him. She says, "Is there somethin— Are you ill this week?"

He says, "No, I'm fine."

She says, "Well, you can stay in this room."

She had a large, large house.

So, he's biding in the room that night when he hears speaking. He looks out the room and he sees the shadow – and it was just the double of hisself – walking with his sweetheart, and kissing her, and speaking about their wedding, and what they're doing.

John was angry.

The shadow comes into John's room and John fights with him. He says, "What do you think you're *doing*? Taking over my whole life now? You're doing everything I— you're taking over!" He says, "I'm not the person I was. I'm getting weaker and weaker and weaker, and you're getting stronger and stronger."

The shadow says, "Well, John," he says. "You are the good side. And I'm your evil side. I *am* stronger than you are. And I'm going to take over."

Rich John was in a dilemma now. He realised this was some evil thing that was taking him over, almost like a doppelgänger. It was taking him over. And he realised that the evil in the shadow was more powerful than what he was. And John now was beginning to turn sickly. He spent many many hours in bed. He couldna hardly get up.

The day of his wedding comes. He's getting very pale and white. And he hears all the joyous celebrations, hears folk saying, "Well, today Rich John and this lassie's getting married, who's very wealthy." And he hears the churchbells ringing. And he kent that the shadow had married the wife. And John was awfa sad.

So, that night, John gets a knife – he's so weak – and he says, "I will *destroy* the shadow." So, that night, the man and his wife come in, and they were lying in their bed sleeping, the man and the wife, and John, very faintly, sneaks in. And he gets this knife and he stabs it into the heart of his shadow.

But, at that point, he finds hisself fading away. And suddenly the shadow wakens up and pulls out the knife. And in a minute or two later, the shadow was whole, and he laughed, and he looked at *his* shadow beside him and he says, "Well, Rich John. Your riches canna help you now. Because I, the evil side, have taken over. *I* was the shadow, but now I am the man, and you have become the shadow." And the evil side won. The evil shadow became John. And he was very wealthy and lived and did many evil things. And poor John faded into oblivion.

THE STOLEN WINDING SHEET

Fran Flett Hollinrake

A long time ago on the island of Sanday there lived an old
woman named Baubie Skithawa. Towards the end of her life
she began to set her affairs in order and was most particular that
everything should be done properly. She got everything ready
for her death, even to the extent of choosing the clothes in
which she wanted to be buried. That summer she had bought a
beautiful winding sheet at the Lammas Fair in Kirkwall, and she
left instructions that her body was to be wrapped in it before
she was placed in the grave. When she eventually died, it was
said by the women who dressed her corpse that they had never
seen finer grave clothes than those of old Baubie.

As was traditional, the neighbours watched over the body for
two nights. There was a woman there called Black Jock, a rough,
coarse sort of woman who was thought to be close kin to the
Devil himself. She had few friends, and folk were scared to cross
her. At the wake, Black Jock was seen touching the winding
sheet, and was heard to mutter, "It's a great pity to put such a
fine piece of cloth in the ground."

Two nights after Baubie was buried, Black Jock took a spade to the Cross Kirk graveyard. She dug up Baubie Skithawa's grave, broke open the coffin lid and took the fine winding sheet off the poor dead body. Then she filled up the grave again and went home. She hid the stolen winding sheet away at the bottom of her wooden kist.

The next day, a young lad named Andrew Moodie was out on an errand. As he was coming back in the murky dusk, the sky grew blacker and blacker and he hurried to get home. He was halfway there when the storm broke – lashing rain, thunder and lightning, the fiercest storm he had ever seen. He saw fire leaping from cloud to cloud. The flashes were nearly blinding. The sea roared and the thunder shook the earth so violently that he was thrown to the ground. Ahead of him lay the kirkyard, and the tempest seemed to be raging even more fiercely there. Raising his head for a moment, Andrew saw a sight that nearly turned him mad with terror.

From every single grave in the kirkyard there rose a mast of fire. They were all colours – red, yellow, blue – and the tops of the pillars were far above the church roof. Some stood straight, but others swayed from side to side, and on top of every one of these pillars of fire stood the spirits of the dead, fluttering in their grave clothes. Some had one, others two or three, huddled together. The spirits beckoned and waved and howled to one another, their shrouds whipped by the wind. There, on top of one of the fiery pillars, he saw one poor forlorn spirit standing motionless and alone and completely naked. Here was the spirit of poor old Baubie Skithawa, whose winding sheet had been stolen. The other wraiths were screaming and pointing at poor Baubie as she hung her head in shame and despair. She lifted her head towards Andrew, and he fled for his life, for he knew that if he looked into her eyes he would surely lose his mind.

Andrew made for the nearest house as fast as his trembling legs would carry him, and screamed and banged and kicked on the door with all his remaining strength. It so happened that the house belonged to Black Jock, and she knew that the spirits were angry about something. In a moment of rare charity, she opened the door and took Andrew in out of the wild night. She banged the door shut again and barred it with the wooden yoke she used for carrying water pails, into which she had embedded three steel spikes. Turning to Andrew, she demanded to know what the Devil he was doing out on such a night.

The moment that she said the Evil One's name there came a clap of thunder right over the roof and such a blaze of lightning that Andrew was both stunned and blinded for a moment. When he recovered, he saw Black Jock sitting in the middle of the floor, drawing circles around her with a big needle. Her lips were moving and her face was dark and troubled. Andrew was about to tell her what he had seen at the kirk, but she threw a hard peat at him and he yelled with pain. She hushed him and bade him listen. Outside, between the crashes of thunder, there came the noise like the shrieking of a thousand scolding souls. They spoke no earthly tongue.

The smokehole, the window and the eaves at the top of the door had all been blocked by Black Jock, but Andrew watched in horror as ghostly hands began to push through. He saw the white and ghostly face of Baubie Skithawa's spirit glowering through the window-hole. The spirit cried mournfully, "Cold, cold am I this night! Cold, cold am I! Give me my sheet! Give me my sheet! It's cold, cold, to lie in the earth, naked! Give me back my sheet!" And then she shrieked fit to rend the heart of any living creature. One of the spirits thrust in his hand through the smokehole and tried to pull away the bar across the door. It shrieked and let it drop at once, for it had touched the steel spikes that Black Jock had put there to ward off evil spirits. The ghosts set up an inhuman roar and began to rage around the house, beating on the roof and the walls.

Finally, Baubie's head, neck and arms burst through the window and immediately the spirit began searching and tearing the house apart. Her arm swept over Andrew, and he cowered down in mortal fear as she struck the top of his head. He fell to the floor, and the toe of his shoe caught Black Jock's hand as she sat with her needle, frantically invoking spells. The needle flew from her hand; she swore a fearful oath. Andrew knew little of witchcraft but he knew that the steel had protected her and now she was powerless. Black Jock flew across the room, flung open her wooden kist and dragged the winding sheet out from the bottom. It was torn from her hands, whirled round and round her head, and whipped out of the smokehole in a blaze of blue fire.

"The Devil himself go with thee and bide with thee!" cursed Black Jock as the sheet switched out of the hole.

From nowhere, an invisible force struck her from behind, flinging her flat on her face on the earth floor.

At that very moment the cock crew, and the spirits were forced to retreat to their own world once more. Andrew Moodie, lying helpless, managed to raise his head and look around at the devastation. In the light of dawn, the damage became clear. Everything was smashed, the roof broken and the doors hanging off. Black Jock lay motionless on the floor. A while later, neighbours came by to help and they found three cows dead in the byre. They picked up Andrew and discovered that on his head was a spirit mark, where Baubie had struck him, no doubt.

Together, Andrew and the neighbours tried to lift Black Jock from the ground where the spirits had flung her. But despite all their pulling, they could not budge her, although five women and three men tried with all their strength. One woman gave the opinion that Black Jock was spirit-bound, held down by some unearthly power. The ghost-cramp, others called it. Fearing what the minister would say, they sent for an old fellow called Mansie Peace, who was thought to be wise in matters otherworldly. When he arrived, he walked around Black Jock seven times, and muttered seven incantations over her. Still she did not move. Then he boiled seven bluestones and made enchanted water of the brew, and poured it all over Black Jock's back. Finally, she managed to rise to her feet.

Black Jock had learned her lesson. Andrew went home, trembling, none the worse for his experience. Although, it was said, on the place on his head where Baubie Skithawa's spirit had struck him, no hair ever grew again.

THE INHERITANCE

Chris Edwards

I inched the car up the overgrown driveway, telling myself that it was the state of the track that was making me slow to a crawl. But no, it was simply being here. With nanna gone, Appledrake was now mine, along with everything else collected by the family over the generations. The trees formed a screen against the road and the rolling hillside so that you were almost on the place before you even got a glimpse of it. Red sandstone overgrown with ivy, the bare bones of a conservatory with an ancient apple tree growing up through broken ribs, the dry fountain in the courtyard surrounded by snarling stone lions.

I brought the car to a stop on the gravel and kept my gaze lowered, engine still running. I looked at the dashboard, the steering wheel, anywhere except the place itself. I tapped out a beat on the wheel with my fingers, deciding if I really wanted this. *Estate, house and all contents*: that was the deal, but it was all or nothing. I could have refused, of course, gone back to my own cosy, cramped little apartment, all bookcases and bicycles and barely room to breathe.

The Inheritance

My mother had wanted to make sure that I was capable of functioning on my own. The last money I'd received from the family had been for my university fees, and my poetry major meant I relied on tutoring and occasional bar work to pay the rent. I counted myself lucky; living in a college town means that there are diversions of both the mind and utter mindlessness, and I had sampled both as the fancy took me. Still, as the years rolled on, I found my circle of friends shrinking, picked off by the ravages of career or domesticity. Lately, I'd had a harder time reconciling my self-image of care-free independence and the reality that I was borderline broke and lonely.

No, as well not pretend – the decision had been made. I turned off the ignition, got out of the car and stared at Apple-drake head on. I took a deep breath, the air heavy with autumn scents from the reddening leaves.

My own memories of the place were from almost two decades ago, one last summer visit with mum. My mother and I used to come down once a year and stay for a week, but even then I could tell it was more like an obligation than a vacation. Mum always spent that week hiring local contractors to do repairs, restocking the cupboards and airing the place out. I realise now that she was trying to reassure herself that nanna was still going strong, putting off her inheritance as long as possible. I guess the joke was on her, because nanna outlived her by many years.

She was a tough old bird, my nanna. In my mind's eye she's never without a cigarette or a glass of gin in hand. She didn't say much, just let mum fuss around her like a crocodile tolerating a plover bird cleaning its teeth. Maybe it was because she was the one person that made mum nervous that I liked her.

It was on that last trip, while mum was off seeing about getting the gutters cleaned or something, that I actually began to believe in all the inheritance business. I don't want to give you the impression that my family were like a cult or something – I wasn't born believing this stuff. Sure, mum told me, but I just figured it was like church – you sit there on a Sunday because that's just what people do. Nobody expects actual miracles or to meet Jesus or anything.

I was wandering about the upper storey of Appledrake. Mum had given me a pair of brand-new yellow gardening gloves and tasked me with tearing off the ivy covering the upper windows. Many of the windows were warped shut from years of water damage, and I was quite enjoying exerting my muscles to force them open. Suddenly I heard the sound of running water coming from nearby. Being the only person around, I dropped the sweaty gloves and tracked it to its source, a tiny bathroom probably originally intended for servants. A tap was flowing full force, water already threatening to overflow the basin of the sink. Instinctively, I went to turn it off, and as I did so my hand brushed the surface of the water and I suddenly felt… regarded. It wasn't terrifying, by any means, but in a way I can't exactly describe I felt very certain that someone, or perhaps more accurately some*thing*, had just introduced itself to me.

Suddenly the penny dropped and I backed away, mouth open. The inheritance was real. It had seen me – *touched* me. I went to one of the windows overlooking the courtyard where my mum was dickering with a bearded workie in a sleeveless high-vis shirt down by the fountain. I banged on the window until she looked up, and suddenly the fountain beside them both burst into life, blasting out the chunks of weed and mud that had choked it up for many years and drenching them both in filthy water.

Nanna hobbled out with a towel a few moments later, grinning ear to ear, and looked right up at me. Thinking about it now, I wonder if she knew that my mother would never inherit, that Appledrake would come to me next? I laughed out loud as the big man swore and slipped in the mud. Mum's eyes were glued to the house, a mixture of fear and aggravation that only grew worse as she saw me smiling. Later that night I heard her arguing with nanna. I couldn't make out the specifics, but I could hear the note of hysteria in mum's voice.

We left early that year, and she didn't take me with her the year after – I was old enough to stay home by myself, and had an enjoyable week of pizza, pot, beer and boys instead. The year after that I was working the summer while I was at university. Mum never offered, and truth be told I'm not sure I would have been able to locate the place by myself. Nanna had no phone, and it seemed we weren't the sort of family who kept up with each other by letter. She never left Appledrake, and I was too busy being a teenager to notice that she'd slipped out of my life.

Now, I stepped onto the porch, noting the warped floorboards, and tried the key in the lock. It turned happily enough, and the door opened smoothly. I ghosted through the halls, everything dust sheets and ancient yellowed photographs. From above the mantel the daguerreotype of the founder of our little clan shows a short woman glowering down from the foothills of the Pyrenees. Too proud to learn French, it was her I had to thank for interminable Occitan lessons as a child.

A noise startled me from my reverie; a dry, fluttering, scratching noise of distress from the study. Steeling myself for the worst, I turned the handle and then let out a breath of relief as I saw it was nothing more than a pigeon that had flown in through a broken window and was batting itself feebly off the glass, trying to escape.

"Come on, you stupid cushie-doo. Let's let you out."

I went over to the window and unfastened the latch. The poor thing was too exhausted to even struggle as I picked it up. I was just preparing to post it outside when suddenly I heard a voice from behind me.

"Please, Bernadette. I am hungry."

There had been no footsteps. In a house as old and creaky as Appledrake I'd have heard for sure. The bird lay nestled in my hands. It was a woman's voice I'd heard. *It* had a woman's voice. Slowly I turned around; slowly I lifted my gaze until I saw two eyes of piercing aquamarine, a face half hidden in shadow in the doorway. I could see enough of her expression to read the look of hunger as she regarded the frail little bird in my hands.

"*Please*, Bernadette."

I looked down at the bird. I could feel the beat of life in that little chest, the fragility of the bones beneath my fingers. I knew what it wanted. I knew what it was asking.

Gently, I laid a hand around the pigeon's head. It had entered that queer state animals find where they know death has come and that struggling will make no odds. People are not so sanguine or sensible.

Those aquamarine eyes regarded me as I made my decision, but, as I said before, that die had already been cast when I accepted Appledrake and everything else. With a swift wrench I snapped the little bird's neck and held it up to the thing in the doorway.

"Aquero, I offer you this life and I ask for your blessing."

The figure closed its eyes for a second, as if sampling a rare vintage, and then opened them again.

"You have my blessing, Bernadette, and my thanks."

But I noticed the look of hunger hadn't abated much. Mentally I made a note – pigeons weren't going to cut it for long.

I heard a rattling in the pipes and, as I'd seen once before in my teenage years, the fountain in the courtyard burst into life, jets of water arcing into the late-afternoon sunlight. She – it – seemed to relish the play of water, those eyes of hers mesmerised by the sight.

"How soon?" I asked it.

"Soon."

Of course she was hungry – it had been almost a month since nanna had passed. Obviously she saw the look on my face because she smiled as she stepped out and wrapped those thin arms around me in a gentle embrace.

"Don't worry, Bernadette. My blessings will protect you for as long as you feed me. I have seen Popes send whole armies to wage slaughter on Languedoc and fail to harm me or my chosen companions. Perfecti cast themselves into the flames rather than speak of me to the Dominicans. Such is my covenant with you and your line – you shall suffer no harm."

"As long as you are fed?"

"As long as I am fed, yes."

The water pipes rattled all over the house, as if Appledrake was a great beast awakening after a deep slumber, or the sap rising in a tree as spring came again.

I was home. At last.

THE POSSESSION

Sean Wai Keung

1

who knew hungry ghosts could exist this far north

i see them sitting high on top of the old walls in glasgow
eyes wide and pale – mouths gaping toothlessly
gossiping with each other about *love island* im told

most people claim they dont exist
while some others go too far the other way
they fall in love with the hungry ghost realm
and raving mad they do things like appear on tv for rambling
interviews or postgraduate studies

the history of scotland is a history of slavery these lunatics say
now they have returned to avenge themselves

but thats not really why the hungry ghosts are here
i know this because i asked one once in merchant city
it confirmed to me that revenge is the last thing on their minds

the possession

if we kill you all
you will only become hungry ghosts like us
then you would haunt us forever
no — better to just let you all get on with yourselves

i asked back *so why are you here then*
but the hungry ghost just laughed and turned its head away
from me

2

the hungry ghost i talk to the most goes by the name robert
allason
he always sits slightly away from the groups of others and is
always up
for a chinwag — *robert allason* i say to him one evening
is it true that hungry ghosts watch and enjoy love island

robert allason nods affirmatively
love is what hungry ghosts miss the most about being alive

its not food i ask back disbelievingly
robert allason mumbles something under his ghosty breath
i cant hear it but i get the impression he knows something
secret

he doesnt want to tell me
but he eventually will

3

during summer hungry ghosts become stronger than normal
whereas in the winter they wither somewhat in the cold
during warmer weather they radiate and grow taller

this makes it even more perplexing to me why they would be
in glasgow
surely they are better suited to far warmer places

i ask robert allason this during another evening
while he lounges on a bank by the clyde
his spectral head lolls around lifelessly as he gives me a puzzled
look

they are here because i am here he says
in a manner suggesting i should already know this

4

the term 'hungry ghosts' comes from the buddhist concept
餓鬼
which itself is a translation of the sanskrit word प्रेत
wikipedia defines the term as representing
"beings who are driven by intense emotional needs in an
animalistic way [...] The term is not to be confused with the
generic term 'ghost', i.e. the spirit of a deceased ancestor. The
understanding is that all people become such a regular ghost

when they die, and would then slowly weaken and eventually
die a second time. Hungry ghosts, by contrast, are a much more
exceptional case [...] It is believed that hungry ghosts can arise
from people whose deaths have been violent or unhappy [...]
Hungry ghosts can emerge from neglect or desertion of ancestors" (source: https://en.wikipedia.org/wiki/Hungry_ghost)

5

one day while trying to interview a particularly thick huddle
of hungry ghosts
a lunatic approaches us ranting about tobacco plantations
i ask the hungry ghosts if they know who this lunatic is
the hungry ghosts cackle and shake their heads violently from
side to side
one by one they melt into the earth and vanish

do you mind i say to the lunatic *i was trying to do an interview*
but the lunatic doesnt hear me
the lunatic is in their own world

some nights i get scared i will become a lunatic too
its on those nights i cant sleep

i have forgotten how i came to be close to the hungry ghosts
now
i only remember arriving here

as soon as i got off the megabus there they were
i couldnt help but see them
watch them
talk with them

i asked everyone i met about them
but they all accused me of being crazy
apart from the lunatics of course but all they cared about
was the realm they occupied
the history they personified
the analysis of their being
they didnt seem to want to get to know them
on any kind of individual basis

6

towards the end of summer i begin to realise that robert allason
may not actually be a hungry ghost but just a regular ghost

i get the hint one day as i walk down towards
one of robert allasons regular haunts

as i turn the corner of hope street i see him
being held in place on the ground by one hungry ghost
his head forcibly pressed up against a giant pale sword
at the end of which two other hungry ghosts stand tall
all four of their hands grasping around the hilt
they laugh but it isnt their normal cackle

this is something more forceful
more genuine

robert allason i shout *whats happening*

and then the sword comes down
and as it pierces robert allasons face
the hungry ghosts leap on him
and out of nowhere a light flashes
like a sudden lightning strike
and the hungry ghosts
and robert allason
are gone

7

according to wikipedia robert allason was
"a Glasgow merchant. Allason was a local man who had begun
life as a baker, before setting up with his brothers in Port
Glasgow as a trader. He made his fortune trading with Britain's
American colonies, eventually becoming a land holder in the
Caribbean. The profits from trade in both tobacco and slaves
allowed him to purchase Flenders Farm (land his family had
worked for centuries)" (source: https://en.wikipedia.org/wiki/
Greenbank_Garden)

8

i begin to ask hungry ghosts i meet about robert allason
most of them try to avoid the question
attempting instead to turn the conversation towards *love island*
some simply stare at me blankly
a couple grow immediately angry and fade away from me

in desperation i attempt dialogues with some of the more
approachable lunatics
i share my theory of robert allason just being a regular ghost
and they agree with me that this is possible

its the only thing that makes sense i say to the lunatics
the hungry ghosts arent here to haunt us
they are haunting him

one of the lunatics tells me i should go to greenbank gardens
since it had been built for the original human-form robert
allason
on flenders farm back in the 18th century

come with me i say to the lunatics
but the lunatics says they are too busy
conducting their experiments on ectoplasm

9

the next day

i wake up

and robert allason is there

on my ceiling

10

before i can say anything robert allason rushes down at me
and for the first time i make physical contact with a ghost

his hands grasp the sides of my head
it feels like icicles pinning me in place
like being stapled to a document i never knew i had to sign

he places his face on my face so that our noses touch
his empty eyes fuse into mine

i try to close my eyes but cant
i try to shout from my mouth but cant
i feel all the moisture in me evaporating
i dont want this

you he growls and his eyes become suns
belong my mind begins to blend itself

to me he melts his face even further into mine
and just like that i become lost

11

robert allason is a liar
hungry ghosts dont enjoy *love island* because they miss love
they enjoy *love island* because its a similar realm to their own

during the eight weeks *love island* takes place
the overwhelmingly hetero cis people who take part
spend their time sunbathing and expressing how they feel
they do this in this specific kind of way
that no living person could naturally achieve

occasionally they have to take part in tasks or dates
sometimes they must speak directly into a camera
to some unseen audience beyond their immediate presence

this is what makes *love island* masterful in its depiction
of personalities distilled to buzzwords
for instance
this one is the funny one
this one is the angry one
this one is the scottish one

and as time goes on these personalities slowly break down
the competitors become simulacra of the original

depictions of themselves until the viewer realises that in this
world these characters own nothing
they can do nothing
they no longer belong to themselves
they belong only to a production team
and this production team directs them in feeling
all the things they have to say they feel

i discuss this with the others while sitting on top of the high
walls
i find myself getting progressively more excited along with
them
for the next episode

how will the funny one goof up tonight
what drama will the angry one start
who will the scottish one pick to couple up with

occasionally i see robert allason
but i have been warned to stay away from him now
the others sometimes whisper things to me
about the three i saw before who attempted to kill him
they say that nobody has seen them since
they say that robert allason fought them all
then chained them up somewhere far away

Sean Wai Keung

it was foolishness one says to me
all we can do is wait for him to die a natural death
all we can do is watch him
follow him

so what do we do i ask

best to just get on with ourselves they say

and so we do

BURIED BY THE DEAD

Jen McGregor

They chose a beautiful place to be buried, I'll grant them that. You can't beat the west for scenery. Dense forests, eddying mists, slate-grey lochs, the works.

The faded red phone box flashes past me on my left. I'm almost there. Down the hill, over the bridge, past the tiny whitewashed church where the minister did the services in doom-laden tones. Caravan site on the right, then a stretch of forest, then… there it is. A tumbledown church surrounded by crooked gravestones, all abandoned in favour of the 'new' kirk some time around 1800. Beyond that, a recent extension to the graveyard with just three or four occupied plots. In the spring it's picturesque and carpeted with bluebells. Now, in October, with the light beginning to fade and the fog rising from over by the loch, it's… atmospheric, shall we say?

There isn't a car park or anything, just a dirt layby on the opposite side of the road. I pull in and get out the car. A fine drizzle hangs in the air, not quite committing to being rain. I retrieve the flowers from the back seat. I take a deep breath. Last time I was here was for Dad's funeral. It's taken me nearly eighteen months to work up to this. I cross the road and approach the heavy wrought iron gate.

It's locked.

It's fucking *locked*.

I've driven for six sodding hours to get here, three of those spent sitting in bloody traffic jams, and the bastarding gate is *locked*.

Why is it locked? Why would you even bother to lock a gate out here? Surely nobody for miles around is going to be the slightest bit interested in breaking into a barely occupied graveyard on a damp October evening? The nearest town is about twenty-five minutes' drive. That's a long way to go if you're looking for trouble, and if you're hell-bent on breaking in then a locked gate isn't going to stop you, you'd just climb –

Ah.

That's it.

I'll climb.

The wall isn't very high, should be easy enough, and there are plenty of hand- and footholds. It'll make a mess of my nice black trouser suit, but it can't be helped. I've come all this way and I'm not going home without visiting my parents' grave. Grasping the flowers in one hand, I stick my toes in one of the gaps, push myself up, and find out the hard way that the ground is lower on the other side. If there were anyone around to see me land, my pride would be wounded.

I go to lay the flowers. It's my first grave visit and I don't really know what to do. I feel like I should stay for a while, so I take my time over everything – walk slowly up to the grave, carefully read the inscription, remove the dead flowers left by some other relative, place the fresh flowers in a hastily improvised ritual arrangement. That kills a couple of minutes.

I try to replay the funerals in my mind, but then I decide against it. I think instead about when they were alive. But I think about them alive quite a lot, just in everyday life, so it doesn't feel like the right thing to do at the graveside. I wonder whether I'm supposed to talk to them. I briefly envy religious people who could just bust out a prayer at this juncture. Instead, I chat self-consciously for a minute or two, telling them about what I've been doing since they've been dead. This only serves to emphasise their absence. I stop. It's been less than ten minutes, but it's enough. It's getting dark, anyway. I scoop up the dead flowers, leaving only my fresh ones, and prepare to climb the wall.

The drizzle has taken steps towards becoming rain and the stones are slippery, so I don't think it's a good idea to climb with the flowers in hand this time. I throw them over the wall in a shower of dead twigs and desiccated petals. I freeze. Then I think I hear something on the other side. Then I relax. It's nothing. What can it be? A hedgehog or something. I begin to break back out of the graveyard.

I reach up over the top of the wall, clutching at the mossy stones. As I pull myself up, my long, damp hair falls forward and sticks to my face, and I curse inwardly at not having worn it up. With my free hand I push it back, catching myself in the eye and leaving a smudgy streak of black mascara across my skin. A wordless growl of frustration escapes me.

And that's when I see her.

And that's when she sees me.

She's staring straight at me. Stock still. Blanched. Eyes wide. Face aghast. Watching me, watching *this*, climb out from among the dead.

And she screams. Of course she screams. She doesn't run, *can't* run, the freeze response has kicked in.

I scramble down, panicked noises that are meant to be comforting spilling from my lips, my blood-red lips, why couldn't I wear fucking taupe and butterscotch shades like a normal person, why couldn't I have left my hair dark blonde, dark blonde would look so much less alarming in this situation, she's pointing at the dead flowers, the dead flowers that I threw, that rained over the wall like a prelude to a jump scare, and now I'm babbling at her –

It's all right, it's all right, I'm not dead, look, check my – well, my pulse is notoriously hard to find so maybe don't do that, but look, I'm – oh god, I see your point, my hands *are* cold, really cold, but that's just because I was by the grave for a bit – not my grave! No! My parents' grave, they live here – well, not *live* here, haha, but they *are* here, look, it's that one there, look through the gate, it's that one there, see? Jackie McGregor, Bill McGregor, and I'm their daughter, Jen –

Yes, yes, that is my name below theirs. But only to say I put up the stone! Really! There's no dates or anything and you'd see that if you just look… Maybe you can't see from here, but if you go in and check – no, no, don't scream, *please* don't scream, I'm not trying to get you to go into the graveyard with me, I didn't mean that, I'm sorry –

Look, I've got a car! If I were dead, would I have a car? See, I've got the keys and everything! You've got a backpack, you must be headed for the hostel near Strachur, can I drop you there? Make up for scaring –

She runs. Finds her feet at last and takes off, and the last thing I see as she vanishes beyond the bend in the road is the little Australian flag sewn to her backpack.

I get back into the car. My hand rests on the steering wheel, pale and knuckly. My face in the rear-view mirror is not the most alive-looking face anyone ever saw. The screaming girl may have had a point.

I wonder whether to follow her and make sure she's all right, but I think I've done enough damage for today.

I wonder whether, somewhere in Australia, there's a woman who tells stories of the time she visited Scotland and saw a rather stylish corpse rise from the grave and invite her into an urban legend.

I wonder whether we'll ever do a sequel…

THE CRAVIN

D. A. Watson

Once, upon a midnight bleary, lyin on ma couch, and far fae
   cheery,
Stony broke and feelin rough unto the root of every hair,
There Ah lingered, fingers twitchin; in ma bones there wis an
   itchin,
Formless dread that wis bewitchin, giein me a subtle scare.
"Tis the Fear," Ah muttered sadly, "and it's giein me a scare.
     Jesus Christ, my napper's sair."

See, Ah'd only vague impressions, of last evenin's drinkin session,
Just crazy hazy scattered memories of a night oot on the tear,
Couple swedgers, Jack n Cokes, Jaegerbombs, two packs of
   smokes,
Talkin pish wi random folks, and fallin doon a flight of stairs.
"Whit a riddy," Ah lamented, "fallin doon a flight of stairs.
     No be daein that nae mair."

The Cravin

But even as Ah lay there dyin, skull in bits an nearly cryin,
And believin that Ah'm needin some professional healthcare,
Well, the Cravin comes a-crawlin, even though Ah feel like
    bawlin;
Like a siren song it's callin, for a dug's medicinal hair.
"No again," Ah moaned, clammy haunds aw fisted in ma hair.
        "Cannae dae this anymair."

Ah was thinking, Ah remember, while turning forty last
    December,
Haufway through a pint of Ouzo which Ah swallyed for a dare,
The self-destructive type, that's me, Ah'll smoke and drink all
    that Ah see,
Have seven sugars in ma tea, although it does me disrepair.
Every deadly, luscious poison that will dae me disrepair.
        Quoth the Cravin, "Geez some mair!"

For what is life, if no for leisure? Why deny yerself some
    pleasure?
Like some reefer, and those massive bags of crisps yer meant
    tae share.
Feelin fine for Buckfast wine, coffin nails and cheeky lines;
Tae beer and hoagies Ah'm inclined, and lyin trippin on the
    flair.
Just lyin there, pure oot ma tits, trippin on the parlour flair.
        Quoth the Cravin, "Evermair!"

For, in ma mind, the Cravin's voice, that says, "We've always got
  a choice,
And even though we're fuckin buckled, there's still plenty room
  for mair,
Even though we're feelin shady, like a dusky, doe-eyed lady.
Fuckin yass! It's nearly payday! Cunning plans are in the air!
There's a boy's weekend fae Friday, in the clear West Highland
  air."
     Quoth the Cravin, "That sounds rare!"

Ah, just barely Ah remember, that mad blurry two-day bender,
Wi ma comrades in the Highlands, in wee huts we had tae share.
Plenty bevvy, drugs and smokes, snacks and music, laughs and
  jokes,
A roarin fire, ma worthy blokes, it's an occasion sadly rare.
Wi the passin of the years, such times are gettin sadly rare.
     Quoth the Cravin, "Isnae fair!"

Then on ma couch, bereft, alone, too feart tae check ma mobile
  phone,
The Fear comes creepin in, a hungry beast come oot its lair.
Doon ma spine ah feel a shiver, cause Ah'm thinkin boot ma
  liver,
And the damage Ah delivered, on that weekend, bright and fair.
Dodgin daggers on the Sunday, fae the eyes of wifey fair.
     She's like a fucked-off grizzly bear.

But tae ma tale: it's late at night, Ah'm feelin like a sack of shite,
When tae ma startlement Ah heard slow heavy footsteps on the
    stair.
Ma bawsack crawled wi sudden dread, cause wife and wean
    were long abed,
So who the fuck is that who treads so loud on darkened stair-
    case there?
"Holy Jesus, Mammy, Daddy, who the fuck is that oot there?"
    Need a change of underwear.

Just leaden silence answered back. Nae gravelled voice fae hall-
    way black.
So, tae quell the quakin of ma heart, and end this grim affair,
Cross ma parlour Ah went stridin, cold sweat on ma brow
    presidin,
Hopin there wis nothin hidin, out on shadowed hallway stair.
And Ah telt maself, "It's just a squeaky floorboard on the stair.
    This it is, and nothin mair."

So, tremblin tae ma very core, Ah opened wide ma parlour door,
The breath locked in ma frozen chest and on ma lips a prayer.
Nae restless son sleepwalked abroad, nae prowler wi shotgun sawed,
Nae droolin werewolf, meathook clawed, lurked in the darkness
    there.
"Whit a fanny," Ah rebuked maself. "Of course there's nothin
    there.
    It's just the Fear and nothin mair."

But then, behind, a stealthy sound; wi girly scream Ah spun
    around,
And Ah saw in dim-lit corner, somethin perched upon a chair.
A shadowed figure, hunched and dark, a presence like a hungry
    shark,
That filled ma breast wi terror stark, a boundless horror
    uncompared.
"Isnae real," Ah telt maself in vain, "this horror uncompared.
        Just a flashback, nothin mair."

The darkling demon smiled and sighed, then pinned me in its
    crimson eye.
"We must speak," it said, "for fearful words and wisdom I would
    share.
We should parlay, you and me, of things that are and yet to be.
Of every sin and selfish thought and act, I warn you to beware,
For I'm the thing you call the Fear, so heed my voice and do
    beware."
        Then quoth the monster sittin there...

"You're not a young man anymore, a fact you simply can't ignore,
And your flesh and bones no longer are so readily repaired.
And for all your japes and joking of your drinking and your
    smoking,
Certain death you are invoking, and your family's despair.
Didn't *your* dad die at thirty-nine, and leave *you* in despair?"
        Quoth the Fear, "And you don't care."

The Cravin

The spectre slid across the room, displacin air like fetid tomb,
Till it towered there above me, fixin me in bloody glare.
"Foolish mortal, puerile chancer, how'd you like a dose of
    cancer?
When you're dead, then who will answer to your son's unheeded
    prayers?
Selfish prick," the Fear it whispered. "You know you haven't
    got a prayer.
        Prick I name you, evermair."

Well, how could Ah respond tae that, in underpants so neary
    shat?
Wi the Fear made flesh, and bold as brass, stood in ma parlour
    there.
But though Ah stood there scared and shakin, wi ma heart and
    kneecaps quakin,
Tightened fists ma haunds was makin, and Ah heard maself
    declare:
"Get tae fuck ya buzzkill bastard ye!" Ah loudly did declare.
        "This Ah'll state, and plenty mair."

"Aye, Ah like unhealthy pleasures, and indulgence should be
    measured,
But even then our deaths are random: there's nae tellin when
    or where.
Because it's just yer Donald Duck. The day ye die? It's doon tae
    luck,

Cause even healthy cunts get fucked, wi tumours, heart attacks
and mair.
And Keith Richards is seventy-four years old, and he'll likely
live a hundred mair!"
Quoth the Fear, "You've got me there."

Well, confounded and outsmarted, then the Fear up and
departed,
But tae this day Ah'm haunted by the prophecy it shared.
Cause the Cravin's ever schemin; sordid plans it's ever dreamin.
Come the weekend, let's get steamin, and oor faculties impair!
Aye, the Cravin and the Fear, they make a right perplexin pair.
Wis true that night, and evermair.

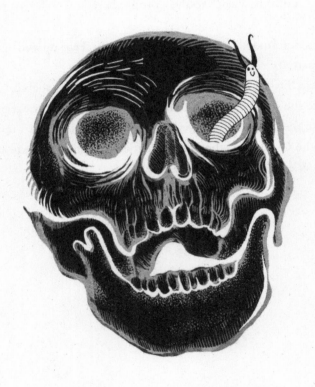

THE SKELETON AND THE GRAVESTONE

Jean Rodger

This is a wartime one.

Two men were working up at the cemetery. As they watched, a skeleton got out of its grave and went away running down the town. And in a wee whiley it came back again and lifted the gravestone and was going away with it in alow its oxter. And they cried, "Here! Where you going with that?"

"Well," says the skeleton, "you canna get anything without your identity card nowadays."

BIOGRAPHIES

Fiona Barnett

Fiona Barnett is an independent researcher and lover of camp-fire stories. Based in Edinburgh, she writes and presents *Past Tense*, an in-depth history podcast on the civil war period of 1625–1660 in the British Isles, as experienced by the English, Scottish and Irish – all of whom did a great line in superstition and ghost stories. The rest of the time, she's a proofreader and high school English tutor.

Paul Bristow

Paul Bristow writes fiction, folktales and comics, sometimes all at once. He has worked for the Scottish Book Trust as a Digital Storyteller in Residence and, as part of heritage group Magic Torch, he has written folktales, ghost stories and comics that celebrate the more unusual history of the West of Scotland and beyond. His first children's book, *The Superpower Project*, was shortlisted for the Floris Books Kelpies prize 2014 and published in 2016, and he has been published in literary magazines such as *404 Ink*.

P. D. Brown

P. D. Brown was born in York in 1957 and grew up in Kendal. In the 1980s he started to rework traditional ghost stories, myths, legends and the early history of pre-mediaeval Britain as stories for oral recitation to live audiences. He has performed, for example, at Caithness Horizons Year of the Ancient Ancestors Festival 2014 and, in 2017, at The Light Club, Burlington, Vermont, USA.

His poetry, mainly in traditional forms, is of the natural world and its decline, and the strangeness of the familiar. Storytelling and prosody have in recent years merged to produce works of narrative verse.

Anna Cheung

As a child, Anna was fascinated by anything weird, spooky or terrifying, and horror stories were no exception. Her unconventional family would huddle together during stormy nights to whisper tales of terror and she would devour every word as they unravelled into the bewitching hours. Among other writings, Anna has continued to explore the dark side of her imagination, spilling Gothic words onto paper. She managed to unleash her spider-ink poetry ('Thirst' and 'Satan's Garden') to crawl across the pages of online literary magazines such as *Dark Eclipse and Dusk* and *Shiver.*

Pauline Cordiner

Pauline is a storyteller from the fishing and farming traditions of North East Scotland and enjoys telling a variety of traditional folktales, legends and anything that chills her bones! Pauline also sings traditional songs and ballads and has been privileged to learn from some of Scotland's most respected Traveller and folk singers. She is the current Chair of the Grampian Association of Storytellers.

Since 2001 Pauline has been performing at science, archaeology and book festivals, Glastonbury Festival, Cambridge and Stonehaven folk festivals, museums, nature reserves and National Trust for Scotland castles as well as local schools and community groups.

Chris Edwards

Chris Edwards is co-creator of and one of the lead voice actors for the audiodrama podcast 'Tales from the Aletheian Society'. He has also written plot and performed roles for numerous acclaimed live-action roleplay events (Projekt Ragnarok, Empire LRP and Incarceration, to name but a few). In his spare time, he enjoys running tabletop roleplaying games for both adults and kids.

Fran Flett Hollinrake

If you'd asked Fran at the age of nine what she wanted to be when she grew up, she would have said "a ghosthunter". While working as a tour guide in the underground streets and vaults of Old Edinburgh, she further developed a taste for the darker side of history, and loves telling tales of ghosts, spectres, witches and scary things.

Fran lives in Orkney. In her work as a tourist guide and custodian of historic monuments, she has surrounded herself with legends, folktales and history, and loves sharing them with others. She gives ghost tours in Orkney's haunted locations and was instrumental in revitalising the annual Orcadian Story Trust. She has never lost her taste for creepy stories.

Gavin Inglis

Gavin's recent writing appears mostly in games, from the undead-next-door mayhem of Neighbourhood Necromancer to the cosmic awfulness of Call of Cthulhu, via the Victorian underworld of Fallen London. His spoken word has graced such venues as a reconditioned porn cinema in Glasgow, a dockers' club in Leith, a festival tent in a field near Ipswich and a glorified steel crate on the beach at Kinlochbervie. He has been to Whitby at least four times and once explained the gothic subculture to a visiting reverend.

Daiva Ivanauskaitė

Daiva Ivanauskaitė is a Scotland-based Lithuanian storyteller. She tells tales inspired by myths and folk tradition from Lithuania, Scotland and other lands. Daiva makes every tale her own, finds parallels with her life and explores themes of identity, environment and togetherness. She performs onstage at festivals and spoken word events, with community groups, with families and in schools. She delivers storytelling workshops, training and courses and also facilitates story work and brings the art of storytelling into organisations. Daiva is the artistic director of Lithuania's first storytelling festival and regularly performs in her native land, her adopted home of Scotland and internationally.

Sheila Kinninmonth

Sheila grew up in a family that told stories. Family gatherings were times when stories were shared and she has naturally continued the tradition, telling stories to her own children and grandchildren, using oral telling during her career in education and honing her skills through the Scottish Storytelling Centre to become an accredited freelance storyteller on the Scottish Storytelling Directory. There is nothing she likes better than sharing her joy of stories with audiences of all ages. She is particularly interested in researching and telling local Scottish folklore and folktales.

Kirsty Logan

Kirsty Logan's latest book is *The Gloaming*. She is the author of three short story collections, two novels, a flash fiction chapbook and a short memoir. Her collaborative work includes 'Lord Fox', a show of spoken word, song and harp music with Kirsty Law and Esther Swift, and 'The Knife-Thrower's Wife', an Angela Carter-inspired album with Kathryn Williams and Polly Paulusma. Her books have won the Lambda Literary Award,

Polari Prize, Saboteur Award, Scott Prize and Gavin Wallace Fellowship. Her work has been adapted for stage, recorded for radio and podcasts, exhibited in galleries and distributed from a vintage Wurlitzer cigarette machine.

Seoras Macpherson

Seoras Macpherson is from Skye and has collected traditional stories from the age of three. His stories come from family traditions passed down through many generations in Skye and Argyll. He has appeared globally on TV and radio and was the first ever Scottish storyteller at the Edinburgh Festival. He regularly performs at storytelling events at home and overseas, is a founding member of the Scottish Storytelling Forum and administers the Isle of Skye Storytelling Festival.

Ali Maloney

Ali Maloney was raised with video nasties in the news and Batman licensed as a breakfast cereal... and it shows. He has performed on stages as diverse as T In The Park and the Sonic Arts Expo in Plymouth, from live sessions on New York's top alternative radio station, WFMU, to Edinburgh and Glasgow horror festivals. His theatre shows include the bleak panto *Ratcatcher* and the diluvial romp of *Hydronomicon*. Currently, he co-hosts the weird art cabaret *Anatomy* and runs the ritualistic horror podcast 'Caledonian Gothic'. 'Brilliant' (BBC Radio Scotland).

Daru McAleece

Daru is a Druid storyteller, performer and artist with the TRACS Scottish Storytelling Forum. He performs around Britain, and his work – informed by a love of myth from Britain, Ireland and around the world – is interactive, exploring inspiration and creativity within individuals and communities. He is interested in exploring and discovering new collective narratives, and often uses storytelling within eco-therapy for adults and children, raising awareness of the natural world around us. His passion for the Gothic stretches back to childhood, all the way from early comics, and his tales and scribblings have always been tinged by this world.

Conner McAleese

Conner McAleese's debut novel, *The Goose Mistress*, details Eva Braun's descent into madness during World War Two. His first short horror story, 'Polite', was included in Dark Ink Press's anthology *Fall*. His next projects include a PhD investigating how horror during the 1970s reflected the cultural anxieties of a post-Counter Culture America and creating a name for himself in performance storytelling.

Jen McGregor

Jen McGregor is a playwright, spoken word artist and Gothic -heroine-turned-monster. Her poetry, essays and fiction have been published in *New Writing Scotland*, *404 Ink*, *Marbles Mag* and *Bare Fiction*. Jen's plays and spoken word performances draw heavily on horror and Gothic fiction and she has featured at Inky Fingers, Interrobang?!, Hidden Door, Bona Fide and the List Hot 100 Party. Her solo show, *Grave*, has been programmed at Flint & Pitch Presents, In the Works Theatre and the Scottish Poetry Library.

Paul McQuade

Paul McQuade is a writer and translator from Glasgow, Scotland. He has told his stories to audiences in Scotland, from the bar to the dissection room (literally), working with material from Scotland's oral and Gothic traditions. He is co-author, with Kirsty Logan, of *Hometown Tales: Glasgow* (Orion, 2018), author of short story collection *Between Tongues* (Cōnfingō, 2020) and recipient of the Austrian Cultural Forum Writing Prize.

Ricky Monahan Brown

Ricky Monahan Brown is the producer and co-founder of the irregular night of spoken word and musical entertainment Interrobang?! (Saboteur Award winner, Best Spoken Word Night in Britain 2017, and Bella Caledonia's Top Scottish Alternative Media for 2018).

Ricky's memoir, *Stroke* (Sandstone Press, 2019), had *The Scotsman*'s reviewer "wincing and cradling her head [after] comparing the brain to a cauliflower and imagining it cut in half, as the author advises the reader to do to explain one procedure". It's also "an inspirational story with a fascinating, and unexpected, ending" (Professor Sir Kenneth Calman).

Alycia Pirmohamed

Alycia Pirmohamed received an MFA from the University of Oregon and is currently a PhD student at the University of Edinburgh, where she is studying poetry written by second-generation immigrants. Her forthcoming chapbook, *Faces that Fled the Wind*, was selected by Camille Rankine for the 2018 BOAAT Press Chapbook Prize. Alycia was a 2019 recipient of the 92Y/Discovery Poetry Contest and, in 2018, she won the Ploughshares' Emerging Writer's Contest in poetry.

Gauri Raje

Gauri Raje is an anthropologist and storyteller who works in the UK and India with adults and vulnerable groups and performs regularly across the UK, India and Europe. Her performance projects include directing 'East of the Sun, West of the Moon', translated and told in three Indian languages, 'Badlands', storytelling of folk stories of the land and rivers of central India, and 'Tales of Exile and Sanctuary', exploring themes of exile. She has researched and co-written a book with biographical and traditional stories of South Asian migrants to the West of Scotland with AwazFM, a South Asian radio station in Glasgow.

Jeannie Robertson

Regina Christina Robertson is a towering figure in Scottish traditional arts, especially in song. Born in Aberdeen in 1908, her Traveller family were already known for their musicianship and singing, and Jeannie inherited and expanded upon an already vast repertoire, fond in particular of relating the stories behind songs she performed. In 1953, Jeannie's local reputation led to her discovery by folklorist Hamish Henderson, setting her on a path of international prominence as a bearer of tradition. Jeannie performed and recorded across Scotland and internationally, both traditional and original material, and in 1968 was awarded an MBE – the first Traveller and first folksinger to be given this honour – for services to folksong.

Stanley Robertson

Stanley Robertson, nephew of Jeannie Robertson, was a ballad singer, storyteller and piper. Born in 1940 in Aberdeen to a Traveller family, he spent much of his working life in Aberdeen fish houses, where he continued to collect traditional material. Stanley appeared regularly at storytelling festivals, published several books, including two volumes of stories and ballads with fellow Traveller and traditional performer Duncan Williamson, and featured in a huge number of radio and TV programmes. From 2002 to 2005 Stanley was a research fellow and keyworker for the 'Oral and Cultural Traditions of Scottish Travellers' project at the University of Aberdeen, receiving an honorary degree in 2008, and represented Scotland at the Smithsonian Institution's Folklife Festival in Washington, D.C. Stanley died in 2009. In recognition of his importance as a storyteller, the Grampian Association of Storytellers awards its 'Stanley Robertson Award for Traditional Storytelling' annually.

Jude Reid

Jude read *Frankenstein* at an impressionable age and has been infatuated with Gothic horror ever since. She lives in Glasgow and writes horror stories in the narrow gaps between her day job, chasing her kids and trying to tire out a border collie. She is co-creator of the audiodrama 'Tales from the Aletheian Society', studies ITF Tae Kwon Do and drinks a powerful load of coffee.

Jean Rodger

Jean Rodger was born and brought up in Forfar, Angus. She attended South School in Forfar and then Forfar Academy before spending most of her career as a teacher at Forfar's East School. Through recordings with Dr Emily Lyle in July 1976, Jean preserved a wealth of traditional material she recalled from life in Forfar, particularly childhood and playground songs and games.

Max Scratchmann

Max Scratchmann is a late-in-life exhibitionist and owner of the secret identity of Bard of Burlesque. As well as being the crazed genius behind the Edinburgh spoken word theatre company Poetry Circus shows, he is a writer, performer, life model and general theatrical dogsbody in his own right, not to mention someone clinging grimly to the now-fading title of award-winning illustrator. He is available for festivals and events in his persona of Professor Max – Takeaway Poet.

Sean Wai Keung

Sean Wai Keung is a Glasgow-based poet and performer. He was a 2017 Starter Artist at the National Theatre of Scotland during which he worked on spoken word and performance representations of takeaway food. He has performed live at venues such as Summerhall, Rhubaba Art Gallery and Sonnet Youth and has been featured in livestreamed events at places including St Anthony's Well, Edinburgh, and the ruins of the Jerma Palace Hotel, Malta. He was awarded the 2014 Best Debut Performance award at Farrago Zoo Spoken Word Awards.

D. A. Watson

Novelist D. A. Watson discovered a penchant for poetry when an experiment in spoken word resulted in his Burns tribute piece, *Tam O'Shatner*, which was published in pamphlet form and deemed gong-worthy at the Dunedin Robert Burns Competition in New Zealand and the Falkirk Storytelling Festival. He has since written and performed a handful of other poems including *The Cravin, The Night Afore Xmas, Wasted* and his love letter to the ravenous deid, *AAAAHHHH! ZOMBIES!!!* He can occasionally be found skulking around open mic nights in the vicinity of Glasgow and the west coast.

Katalina Watt

Katalina Watt has a background in spoken word and storytelling performances, most recently as part of the Events team at Golden Hare Books, as well as stage experience as director and cast member of productions with Student Theatre at Glasgow and in various jazz dance troupes. Her fiction has received First Prize for Glasgow University's Creative Writing Society Short Story Competition 2014 and an Honourable Mention for IntroComp 2017, and has been featured in literary anthology *Narissa*, of which she is the creator and editor, and online for the Glasgow Women's Library. She has a forthcoming piece in the 2019 BAME Writers pamphlet published by Tapsalteerie.

Betsy Whyte

Betsy Whyte was born in 1919 in the Perthshire village of Old Rattray. Born into the Townsley Traveller family, famous as crafters and particularly as basket weavers, Betsy lived an itinerant life before settling with her husband in 1939 in the area of Montrose. Known for her sense of fun and humour, fascinating stories and her rendition of the ballad 'Young Johnstone', she achieved wide recognition after coming to the attention of the University of Edinburgh's School of Scottish Studies. Betsy wrote two works of autobiography, *The Yellow on the Broom* (1979) and *Red Rowans and Wild Honey* (1990), before her death in 1988 while attending the Auchtermuchty Folk Festival. She is now widely recognised as a powerful ballad singer, influential storyteller and example of the power of resilience and humour in the face of prejudice. Much of Betsy's work is held by the School of Scottish Studies.

Biographies

Duncan Williamson

Duncan Williamson was a storyteller, singer, writer and one of the legendary voices of Scottish Traveller culture. Born in 1928 in a bow tent on the banks of Loch Fyne, Duncan spent six decades travelling around Scotland collecting stories and songs. Williamson received international recognition during his lifetime, making appearances at literary and folk events, producing audio recordings and writing numerous books, including his autobiography *The Horsieman: Memories of a Traveller, 1928–1958* (1994). He died in Kirkcaldy in 2007. His work is held in numerous archives, including the Center for Appalachian Studies and Services at East Tennessee State University and the Scottish Storytelling Centre in Edinburgh.

Illustrator: Zuzanna Kwiecien

Zuzanna Kwiecien is an illustrator based in Scotland. With her practice she aims to develop bodies of work that capture the visual narrative of the subject and combine it with a distinct atmosphere. Her illustrations usually feature intricate linework and patterns. She enjoys creating pen and ink illustrations with a focus on detail and with foundations in dark folklore.

ACKNOWLEDGEMENTS

A lot of work has gone into this project and it genuinely couldn't have happened without these people, to whom I'd like to give my whole shrivel-hearted thanks.

First and foremost, I would like to thank **each and every storyteller** in this anthology. Their talents are evident. And their enthusiasm and professionalism meant that organising audio recordings and multiple storytelling events was as painless as it could be.

I'd also like to thank the **University of Edinburgh's School of Scottish Studies**, **Cathlin Macaulay** and **Louise Scollay** in particular, for their support of the project and their co-operation and hard work in acquiring permission to reproduce the fantastic stories of Jeannie Robertson, Stanley Robertson, Jean Rodger, Duncan Williamson and Betsy Whyte. Their archive is a true cultural gem and you should all visit it (though not all at once).

Thank you to the **Traveller and storytelling families** who gave me permission to share their stories. It was a privilege and I hope I've done you justice.

To **Zuzanna Kwiecien** for the incredible artwork and for being unbelievably adaptable, professional and generally awesome to work with.

Acknowledgements

To **Iain and Kirsty McKinna at Offbeat Studio** in Edinburgh for their audio expertise and professionalism while recording the audiobook. I hope we didn't leave too many ghosts behind in the studio.

To **Miriam Morris** and **Fiona MacDougall** from the **Scottish Storytelling Forum** for helping to promote *Haunted Voices* to Scotland's storytellers.

A massive thank you to **Caro Clarke, Laura Jones, Heather McDaid** and **Jamie Norman** for their consultations, advice and guidance. Publishing horror was less scary with their wisdom.

I'd like to thank **my doppelgänger** for not assuming my identity and for letting me lead my own life. (Or has my doppelgänger written this?)

To **Kirstyn Smith** and **Katy Lennon**, two kick-ass women changing publishing for the better, for their spooky support.

To **Splon**.

A huge thank you to **Ross Stewart**, for his fantastic work copy-editing the book and transcribing the archived pieces (trained to do so at the School of Scottish Studies itself). *Haunted Voices* could not have happened without him.

Finally, I'd like to thank every single person who backed *Haunted Voices* on Kickstarter, as well as those who wanted to but couldn't. You all rock.

HAUNTLINGS

Thank you to all these people, and the anonymous ones, for backing the project and bringing *Haunted Voices* to life.

ABS
Adam Tinworth
Adam Trauger
Aderyn Kirsten Nielson
Aidan Hanratty
Aiden Clark
Alan Smith
Alastair Dickson
Alexandra Petropoulos
Ali Maloney
Alice Piotrowska
Alice Slater
Alison Donn
Amy Coop
Amy McNee
Andrew Parsons
Anna Tindale
Archie Duncan

Ash Ogden
Ava Dickerson
Barry Hughes
Ben Birrell
Benjamin Hausman
Blue Bear Books
Brandon Lim
Brett Burkhardt
Bruce Easton
Bryony Baines
Cait Charniga
Calder Hudson
Carla Hepburn
Caro Clarke
Carolyn Cook
Casidhe Nebulosa
Catherine Ogston
Cato Vandrare

Catriona Cox

Chiara Bullen

Chris Shuttleworth

Christopher Wheeling

Claire Main

Craig Stewart

D. Franklin

Daiden O'Regan

Dan Hunt

Daru McAleece

David Quantick

Deborah Rea

Deborah Winslow

Denise Cowle

Duncan Jones

Edward MacGregor

Eleanor Abraham

Elizabeth McIvor

Ellen Desmond

Emily Benita

Emma Moyse

Emma van Straaten

Emma Watts

Eric Schaefer

Ewan Mackie

Federica Fiorillo

Fiona MacDougall

Fiona Stewart

Gemma Doran

Gerald Lofstead

Gill Jones

Gina Hilua

Golden Hare Bookshop

Graeme Strachan

Gwendolyn R. Schmidt

Hannah Fields

Harry Murrell

Heather Parry

Heather Perry

Heather Valentine

Heiko Warnecke

Helen Glen

Helena Roots

Henry Tufts

Howard Kistler

Iain Ross

Iain Smith

Ian Maxton

Ian McFarlin

Ian Wilson

India Genack

Jackie Smith

Jade Scard

Jakob Pfafferodt

Jamie Norman

Jan Wojturski

Jane Alexander

Jared Shurin

Jen Cousins

Jennifer Leveillee

Jennifer Porath

Jennifer Wheary

Jenny Kumar

Jesper Mårtenson

Jodie Stocks

John Fulton

John Stewart Watson

Jon Wallace

Jonathan Bell

Jonathan Harden

John Wojturski

Jordin Baugh

Josephine Birch

Jude Reid

Jules Danskin

Jules Fattorini

Kaitlin López

Karen Waldron

Karon Flage

Katalina Watt

Kate Harvey

Katherine Bowers

Katie Lowe

Katy Lennon

Katya Bacica

Ken Dover

Kerri Logan

Kevin Clark

Kirsten Ahern

Kirsten Knight

Kirstin Lamb

Kirsty Andrews

Kirstyn Smith

Laura DeHaan

Laura Elderkin

Laura Hemmer

Laura Jones

Laura Purcell

Lauren Godde

Lauren Livesey

Lauren Nickodemus

Lewis Allen

Liam Doyle

Lighthouse Bookshop

Linda Farmer

Lisa Ciccarello

Lisa-Marie Ferla

Lucy Angel

Mairi McKay

Mara and Breagh Hughes

Marco Johannsen

Marija Katiliute

Mark Chevallier

Mark O'Neill

Martin Boyle

Martin Gleghorn

Martin Gorrie

Martin Woodhead

Mary Dover

Melvin Oosterhuis

Michael Dempster

Michael Richardson

Michael Walsh

Mika Cook

Miriam Morris

Molly Drummond

Morven Gow

Morvern Cunningham

Naomi Farmer

Natasha Campbell

Nathan Benham

Nathaniel Kunitsky

Nathaniel Massman

Neil Chue Hong

Neil McAleece

Nicholas Krebs

Oliver Godby

Ophelie Lebrasseur

Pam Sherman

Paul Childs

Paul D. Jarman

Paul Dulski

Paul McKie

Paul Michael Clarke

Paul Rossi

Paul Sparrowham

Paul Zambrano

Paula Lyttle

Pauline Barclay

Pauline McKee

Perminder Mann

Peter Blackledge

Peter Nielson

Philippa Cochrane

Rebecca Brown

Rebecca Mastromattei

Richard Rossi

Richard W. Strachan

Rigel Meketa

Rita Faire

Robert Bryson

Ross Jamieson

Ross Stewart

Rozalind Holmes

S. A. Rennie

Samuel Best

Sarah Barnard

Sarah Grout

Sarah McDonald

Scott Lyall

Scott Russell

Selene Brown

Serena Kaye

Sha Nazir / BHP Comics

Shaun Higgins

Shayna Christoe

Sian Ellis

Simeon Ewing

Simon James

Simone Hutchinson

Stephanie Wasek

Steven Perry

Stoo Goff

Stuart Goss

Sylvia Pegg

Tanuja Shelar

The Portobello Bookshop

Tim Ereneta

Timothy C. Baker

Tony Wells

Transreal Fiction

Trevor Harbeard

Typewronger Books

Vaneet Mehta

Viccy Adams

Victoria Hill

Victoria Marland

Victoria Syharath

Will Skinner

Winter Curran

Yasmin Hackett

THE CREDITS

Creating a book takes a massive team effort. Haunt would like to thank everyone who worked behind the scenes on *Haunted Voices*.

Managing Director and Editor
Rebecca Wojturska

Copy-editor and Transcriber
Ross Stewart

Designer and Illustrator
Zuzanna Kwiecien

Typesetter
Laura Jones

Contracts Consultant
Caro Clarke

Audio Producer
Iain McKinna

You've **read** *Haunted Voices* (or skipped to the end).

Now **listen** to *Haunted Voices*.

The audiobook features our fantastically spooky stories from the mouths of the storytellers themselves.

www.hauntpublishing.com

@HauntPublishing